"Razor-sharp observations about today's world
and our obsession with clean living and the esoteric."

KIM RIGBY
author of the Black Fire Chronicles series

"This book never winks at the audience,
it treats its unconventional threat as a real danger,
making this one of the weirdest horror
novels I've read recently."

ELFORD ALLEY
author of *High Strangeness*

THE HAUNTING OF HARRY PECK

DAVID-JACK FLETCHER

LETHE
PRESS

ISBN: 9781590217757

Front Cover and Interior Design by Inkspiral Design

Published by Lethe Press
All rights reserved.

For Paul,
always.

The following is a retelling of real events. The source material is plagued with incomplete records. The events depicted in the *Book of Shaman* have been reconstructed based on what evidence could be gathered, including the personal journals of the people involved, and multiple sessions of retrocognition aided by so much pansy tea. A shit ton.

No names have been changed.

PROLOGUE

Book of Shaman:
"The Massacre at Roanoke" Part One

Roanoke, North America, 1585

STORIES WERE TOLD OVER THE high seas as waves crashed against the hull and storm clouds threatened to shipwreck the marvellous *Red Lion*. One of seven ships on the voyage transporting families to a new land. To a new life.

The initial excitement and anticipation had faded a month into the journey after several crates of the voyage's rations had been swept into the ocean's depths by a severe storm. When the transport reached the Pacific's middle, scurvy took hold. With little food and barely enough water for the children, moods began to flare. The crew and the families aboard began to turn on each other.

James White, known around London for his fresh loaves and juicy pies, held his stomach as it rumbled in tandem with the thunder above. Yet another storm was brewing.

His gums had long since succumbed to the rot pulsating from his deteriorating body, but the hunger persisted. His skin had broken out in rashes, and he struggled to open his eyes. Struggle he did, though, for the fear that once he slept, he would not wake. Perhaps his stomach would fold in on itself and eat him from the inside out. Or perhaps the scurvy would kill him between snores.

Instead, he listened to the stories echoing through the lower decks about the life they would live upon arrival in Newfoundland. The so-called great governor Ralph Lane had carved his piece of North America on an island known as Roanoke. The name was mysterious to James White, much like the traditional landowners from whom Governor Lane had stolen the island.

"It's not theft," Lane had said to the sea captain as James passed by one day. "As per our queen, the beautiful Elizabeth, these lands are unclaimed by Christian kingdoms and therefore ripe for the taking."

James listened through his seasickness and fatigue, knowing those stories were the only thing keeping him alive. Stories about the land. Stories about the people. The Indians, though James wondered if they'd named themselves that or just accepted their fate as an anthropological discovery by white men.

The people demonstrated great hospitality or so everyone believed from Sir Walter Raleigh's earlier expedition. Hospitality was perhaps the Indians' first mistake. Their welcoming and generous nature laid the foundations for the subsequent British land claim.

James White disagreed with the acquisition methods, but he was a humble baker and had no right to think such thoughts nor cast judgment over those who knew more of these matters. All he had known for sure was that he could not afford his business in London and that this new world, this Roanoke, was being offered as his salvation.

As a chef, a step above a mere baker, he would be responsible for the hunting parties and food preparation for the soldiers and other settlers. Thoughts of food kept his stomach churning and his eyes open as the ship sailed into the unknown.

Just as his body had given up, relinquishing control to the ravages of scurvy, he heard the tired mumblings of the captain. Exhausted whispers carried through the ship's lower decks, sailing through the infested air like a tonic.

Soon, the whispers became exclamations and raucous cheers. The *Red Lion* had spotted land. The journey would soon be complete.

As weak as the sailors were, they worked together to prepare the ship for arrival. James stayed below deck, clutching his hands under his chin, thanking the Lord in heaven for his mercy. The noises from above were like an angelic choir, signalling their survival and the beginning of a new page in British domination.

He started to dream of the food he would create to thank the sailors and the captain as he made his way to a rowboat that would take him to shore. The land, the beautiful coastline, moved something inside him. Not hunger this time. Something else. His eyes welled up, salty drops cascading into the water around him. The island was within reach now, the lush green of the forest, the wet golden sand mere metres away.

"Mama." A child tugged at a woman's arm. "Is this heaven?"

The mother cradled the child in her arms, weeping and nodding. No words were needed, and the child wrapped their arms around their mama's neck, whispering thanks as James himself had done only minutes earlier.

The grass under his feet was like a thousand tiny needles, sharp and pointy, yet the sensation pleased him. He had made it. His legs wobbled beneath him, not yet adjusted to the unmoving land. The stillness felt strange after months on the rough ocean, developing sea legs, and walking at an angle in rhythm with the swaying tide. James fell to his knees and kissed the wet grass beneath him, sure their troubles were over. His head swelled as his eyes adjusted to the beauty of the land around him. The fresh air, no longer filled with salt or the sounds of seagulls waiting for another passenger to die, washed through him. Now, he smelled the earth. It had a certain power and held a promise for the future.

James felt alive, grabbing handfuls of grass and dirt and rejoicing in the green sprouting under his knees and feet. He was comforted by their arrival despite the scurvy. Despite the knowledge that there was so much still to do.

Others had done the same, kneeling on the wet earth, crying to the heavens in gratitude for their safe arrival to the wonderful Roanoke. Families cheered, and children played with renewed energy and hope. They threw sand at each other, tore leaves from the trees, and danced around as they fell to earth like confetti. They splashed in the water with a laughter James feared he might never hear again.

Their joy was short-lived, though, as their scurvied lungs caused them to cough and choke.

In the following months, James regained health and strength and undertook his cooking duties with pleasure. Everyone appreciated his efforts, despite only eating what the Indians had been forced to hand over. Nobody talked about the dwindling numbers of Indians or the increasing rarity of their visits. Nobody talked about the bodies that were often found half-buried and rotting by the tree line.

The focus had always been on the survival of the colony. Its ability to eat. The hunting trips had been too much for James to bear upon arrival, but as his health repaired, so did his confidence that he was ready to take up arms and make some real British stew.

"I want to join the hunt," James pleaded to Mack, the hunting leader.

Mack cast a wary eye over James, sizing him up as though he were the next meal. With upturned lips, Mack asked why the chef would want to hunt.

"It — it's what I-I was supposed to be doing all along," James stuttered, biting his lower lip. "I-I need to earn my keep here."

Mack leaned in close to the young man, breath thick on James' face, and slapped him hard on the back. "Welcome to the party, son."

Perhaps through serendipity, the next hunt was that same night. James gulped with fear as he trudged through the woods on Roanoke's outskirts, musket heavy in his arms. It was nice to be part of the team, to feel like his presence was worth a damn, but the sounds of native wildlife scurrying in fear made James doubt their purpose. Before now, he'd never considered that his ingredients had once been alive. He'd never thought of them as creatures with hopes and dreams. Now, it was all he could think about. Couldn't they eat plants instead of living creatures? Who said the fresh carcasses of animals were the best source of protein, anyway? Where did that myth come from?

The thoughts echoed in his brain as Mack pulled him to the ground, taking shelter behind a thick, fallen tree branch.

"This one is yours," he whispered, helping James aim.

"Maybe you can —"

"Quick," Mack interrupted, "else it'll scamper away."

James eyed his prey: a raccoon fiddling with twigs in the grass, unaware of the danger lurking just feet away.

Mack whispered again, his spittle wetting James' ear. Rubbing the spit on his shoulder, James took aim. Held his breath.

As he squeezed the trigger, the raccoon looked at him, its black eyes round with a sudden, intense jolt of fear. In the blackness, James saw its soul. He saw the evil he'd perpetrated.

The raccoon fell to the grass, a mess of red fur and intestines.

"Ha!" Mack smacked his back again, jumping up with glee. "He'll make a fine hat!"

James decided not to remind the man that he had three raccoon hats already. Instead, he nodded and feigned a smile.

As the hunting party continued its killing spree, slaughtering raccoons, squirrels, and whatever else moved,

James knelt over the unmoving body of his victim. At that moment, he swore he would never take another life. Mack scooped up the raccoon and threw it in a netted bag with the rest of the kills, telling James that the hunt was over.

He counted seventeen animals. Dead. All dead.

The hunting party made its way back to camp, not a care in the world, James trailing behind. In the wilderness, a horrible scratching tore at his heart. Looking at Mack's bag of animal loot, the corpses bumping up and down with each step, James knew.

The scratching was just the beginning.

PART I

ONE

2016

THE SHOTGUN WAS HEAVY IN my arms, tucked firmly into my shoulder. I blinked sweat from my eyes, trembling, conscious that my deep breaths were the loudest thing for miles. Raising the weapon, pre-loaded and ready to go, I held my breath.

My heart thumped. I knew this was it. Me or him – isn't that how these things go? One of us had to survive, and it might as well be me. I had a lot to live for – at least, that's what I told myself as I stared down the barrel of the gun. Target in sight.

He looked straight at me, those eyes piercing the core of my soul. Like he knew it was coming. Like he understood. He was scared, moving around the grass to avoid my aim. I faltered at the low cluck echoing in my ears.

He's begging, isn't he? He wants to live. He has a family.

Thoughts raced through my mind as the shotgun grew heavier. I could smell the gunpowder and taste the metal. The trigger seemed sensitive, and I shifted my finger away from it.

The *cluck-cluck-cluck* kept coming from all over the yard. It wasn't just him. It was the whole village. They had all turned to stare at me, their panicked clucking tantamount to prisoners on death row asking for one final chance. The innocent ones who the cruel injustices of the system had let down.

"I can't do this." I threw the gun to the grass and started to walk back to the house.

My uncle's hand gripped my shoulder, stopping me in my tracks. "Come on, Harry. They don't know what's happening."

I turned around and stared at the chickens and roosters in the pen, their tiny eyes wide with fear and anticipation of their impending murder. They didn't know who was next, but they did know what was coming. And there was nowhere to hide.

This whole exercise just seemed so pointless. Making me shoot a chicken. It would demonstrate manhood or masculinity or whatever, so I was told. Uncle John had almost choked on his scotch the night before when I'd said I had never held a gun nor taken a life, which had led to a pained conversation about rites of passage and no member of the Peck family being a shotgun virgin.

Uncle John returned the gun to my arms and helped me take aim. "Go for the plump fella in the back."

I stepped forward to get a closer look. The rooster seemed unaware, nestled amongst some hay. The soft breeze caressed his little face and flowed through his auburn feathers—a final moment of joy before the boom. I inched closer, heeding my uncle's advice to stay quiet. The others in the yard clucked and screeched, warning their brothers and sisters of the reaper in their midst.

But not this little guy in the back. He didn't have a care in the world. His eyes were closed, and I swear I heard him snoring. What dreams he must have on this beautiful day, and I was about to take it all away.

"That's it," Uncle John whispered. "Aim like that red comb of his marks him as commie."

To my everlasting shame, I raised the shotgun. I was trembling as I did so but aiming nonetheless. I pressed my finger against the trigger, squeezed my eyes shut, and fired, squealing at the force of the weapon's recoil. The bang rang in my ears, and there was no sound for a moment.

His family scattered in the aftermath, wondering who was next.

There were no drawn-out final breaths or painful screeches. One second, he was enjoying the breeze and loving his life as a rooster. The next, I was a thief, stealing his bliss. I was a murderer.

Uncle John was oblivious to the moral toll my action had just taken, slapping my back with pride. "Great shot."

I opened my eyes, holding back the tears and the vomit and the shame, and looked at the murder scene. The animal just lay there, a deep red tarnishing his auburn feathers.

Dropping the shotgun, I ran back to the house, my uncle calling after me.

He was a fowl farmer. Slaughter was his bread and butter. I hadn't given much thought to how my chicken ended up on my plate, or how its backside ended up stuffed with a mixture of breadcrumbs and herbs. Or how the little nuggets were made at McDonald's. I had purchased and then digested thousands of those delicious little chicken pieces without a thought spared for the life I was devouring. The thought of the Colonel's popcorn chicken made my stomach turn as I packed my bag.

"Where are you going?" Uncle John stood in the shadow of the doorway, his greying monobrow furrowed.

"I can't be here." I threw clothes, shoes, and dirty underwear into my bag and zipped it up as fast as possible.

Uncle John blocked the door, arms outstretched in front of him. "What's the matter?"

"Don't you understand?" I screamed. "I'm a monster!"

TWO

THE DRIVE BACK FROM MY uncle's farm was long and arduous, between random downpours of rain and violent outbursts of emotion from me. I'd pulled over three times to vomit, crying to the heavens for forgiveness, spikes of rain mixing with my tears.

The universe was against me. That much I knew for certain as roadside billboard after roadside billboard advertised chicken of every imaginable variation: schnitzels, roast, barbecue, between a bun, and deli slices. I was even rattled by the *If you lived here, you'd be home by now* sign. Home. The chicken didn't have a home anymore. No home, no family, no friends. I'd taken it all away, and for what? To show my uncle I was a man. I'd made a terrible mistake, one that couldn't be undone. And the universe was going to make damned sure that I knew it.

When, at long last, I arrived home, I climbed the stairs to my apartment on the fourth floor, accepting without question that the elevator was out of service. I dragged my suitcase after me, the *thump-thump* against each step echoing in the stairwell.

Then the shadow of a chicken's comb – the daggers atop

the head – appeared in the corner of my eye, and the *thump-thump* of my heart drowned out the *thump-thump of* my bag.

The crimson sun was setting as I entered my apartment, the metal keychain clanging against the door. As I placed the keys in a bowl and hung my coat on the rack, I heard the low sound of scratching. It came from behind the walls.

"Hello?"

I knew it was useless as soon as I said it, but part of me still expected a response. Maybe my neighbour was scratching paint off the wall, as he was known to do. Or perhaps there was no scratching, and my guilt was in overdrive, as it was known to be.

No response came. I was alone. I was *always* alone. A history of regrets and bad choices trailed me.

I walked through my apartment, sniffling, shoulders heavy with regret. The scratching followed my footsteps, under the floorboards this time. I tapped against the wood with my heel. The scratching stopped.

"Great," I sighed. "Just what I need."

Mice. Or, heaven forbid, rats. Either way, me plus vermin equalled a fancy hotel room on the other side of town. And lots of ice cream. But that would have to wait. I was exhausted and fragile, and I felt I deserved rats at that moment. Might as well lock them in a cage and strap it to my stomach like the Europeans used to do to convicts.

I checked my father's wristwatch. The time had ticked around to six-thirty. I often liked to stay up late watching Conan O'Brien or something just as trashy, but not tonight. I couldn't stomach his auburn hair and his pointy nose. It was just too fowl at the moment. Those eyes of his were always wide as if with fear. That hair was like a mass of feathers caught in a windstorm. No, not tonight. I didn't know if I would ever be able to stomach auburn-coloured anything ever again.

I went to bed, ignoring the scratching under my feet as I kicked off my boots and threw my shirt to the floor.

Sleep was a fantasy that night, existing somewhere on a dark horizon, forever out of reach. The red glow of my digital alarm clock persisted through the night, counting down the minutes until daybreak until all the roosters usher in the new day. All but one.

As the sky deepened into a midnight blue, I pulled the quilt up to my chin, sobbing into the down feathers hidden beneath the soft fabric. Even though my victim had not screamed or screeched, I couldn't stop seeing his face enjoying that light breeze. Or the blood oozing from his little heart. I couldn't stop hearing the terrified clucks of his family and friends as they scattered for safety. Echoes of their shrieking, visions of them clawing over one another like children evading the monster from under their bed.

I am the monster.

As I stared at the ceiling, the shadows began warping into strange shapes. The chicken crown, like blades waiting to stab my flesh. A beak formed in the darkness.

I heard the unmistakable sound of a long, slow cluck.

Brrrrrrrkk.

I sank low into the bed, peering at the shadows streaming across my walls. The scratching began once more. Under the bed. Behind the walls. Clawing for an exit like Ryan Reynolds in that movie where he was buried alive.

The scratching grew louder. Splinters of the floorboards floated through the air like pollen. The chicken shadows descended upon me, pecking at me from another realm.

"Stop it, stop it, stop it!" I screamed into the darkness and threw my down pillow at the wall. A tiny pale feather burst loose and rose to the ceiling, which made me scream again.

The scratching stopped. The shadows recoiled and disappeared.

I wiped the sweat from my face and neck, conscious that my sheets were wet, a stain spreading through to the mattress beneath. I lay back against the soaked sheets, panting. It had to have been a nightmare. It couldn't be real. I had found sleep after all, and my guilt had sent me twisted dreams of a mad rooster.

The alarm clock buzzed me out of my catatonia. I wasn't supposed to be back at my uncle's farm for another four days, but in my haste to get there yesterday, I hadn't bothered to turn the damned thing off. As it buzzed, vibrating against the nightstand, I wished I hadn't been so lazy. As I slapped the top of the clock, the room fell silent. I peered around and watched the shadows fade against the rising sun.

"It was a dream," I told myself, letting out a reluctant laugh.

As I slid my legs from beneath the quilt and twisted my body into a sitting position, my bare feet recoiled at something sharp. Taking a closer look, I held a hand to my mouth and shook my head.

Splinters.

A mound of wooden splinters loosened from the wood by the fierce scratching from my nightmare. Except it hadn't been a nightmare. Eyes wide with fear, I noticed something else gliding across the floor, weightless.

A handsome auburn feather.

It landed by my feet, and I touched it, but the feather sank through the floorboards. Before I had time to react, my bedroom door slammed. The scratching began again. This time, it was slow, rhythmic. Closer than the night before.

I crawled back into bed and pulled the covers up to my chin. Ignored the dampness on my backside. The scratching turned to thuds, heavy against the flooring.

"Who's there?" I called as I stared at the door. I watched blood seep out from the wood until it congealed in the shape of chicken feet. Then another, and I began to shudder as a series of bloody footprints came towards me.

I pleaded, shouting my apology for the ultimate sin I'd committed.

The footprints reached the foot of my bed, the gore seeping back through the wood as if they'd never existed. I peered over the edge of the bed, unsure what I would find.

Nothing. No blood. No footprints.

Just me and my soiled bedsheets.

THREE

THE DAY WAS A DAZE of coffee, internet searches, and the incessant beeping of my washing machine. I lived in a tidy, one-bedroom apartment, designed for the on-the-go businessperson though I doubt my work history qualified me as "on-the-go" unless you counted the number of times I'd been sacked and escorted off the premised.

I'd bought the place straight from the plan a few years back, the one time I'd been flush after my father didn't make it out of the Grampian's bushfire.

The *beep-beep* of the washing machine made my sleep-deprived eyes twitch like a lobotomy patient as the pick went in. Except my eyes were fine. My brain was fine, too — which made the events of the night prior even more concerning.

My usual internet browsing history could be summed up by dating sites (I hated my profile pic on BuggerHim!), recipes I'd never cook, and the Bureau of Meteorology. But since that morning, I spent hours searching the internet, searching through site after site about the existence of ghosts, DIY Ouija boards, the utility of herbs and spices in protecting yourself from poltergeists, and a brief history of hauntings in Australia.

When I typed *Can you be haunted by a chicken* into Google, I didn't know what to expect. I sure as heck wasn't expecting a series of blogs and Reddit posts about the manifestation of animal curses that happen when an animal dies violently. In some rare instances, a malevolent spirit is unleashed.

In Germany in 1773, the bodies of a sheep farmer and his family were found in their barn. They had sold wool, but when times had gotten tough, they'd turned to selling the sheep for their meat. The family's bodies had been skinned alive, the sign of the ram painted in blood on the barn door.

France, 1882: a cattle farmer butchered his livestock after a mad cow variant infected the herd. He was found hanging by his feet, beheaded and half-eaten. Detectives on the scene recounted hearing aggressive mooing from a distance despite no cows to be found on any of the neighbouring farms.

There were cases like this all over the world, dating back to the 1600s. One blogger insisted that Hitchcock's *The Birds* was based on the true story of a town torn apart by angry ravens after a mass culling in 1943. Another blogger claimed to have been possessed by the spirit of a goat in 1984, compelling him to devour the neighbour's cat. I ignored the fact that goats don't eat meat, which was a massive flaw in this guy's claim, and wondered if an angry dead goat might feel the desire to eat a cat. With everything else I was reading, it didn't seem too far-fetched.

I kept researching, finding case after case of animal vengeance. My eyes skimmed over repeated references to somewhere in North America. A place called Roanoke. I knew the stories of the disappearing settlement and the mystery surrounding what had happened to the villagers. Believing that Roanoke resulted from an animal haunting was ridiculous. Next, the conspiracy nuts would be saying that JFK's real assassin had been a very unhappy crow.

My stomach growled as I stumbled upon an advice blog offering ways to beat an animal curse. The leading theory was to engage in veganism. According to the site, a haunted person should make amends for their crime by abstaining from carnivorous behaviour. It went further, though. To seek the forgiveness of the animal you wronged, you must become an agent for the animal. Speak for it because it can no longer speak for itself.

I hoped that my haunting would be short-lived now that I had the tools to seek forgiveness.

My stomach growled again, and I reached into the fridge for leftover chicken pesto. I stared into the dish, unsure what to do.

What was the ethical action? I couldn't eat it lest I enrage the chicken-demon further. But could I throw it out? That seemed just as foolish. The animal was already roaming the big farm in the sky, so wouldn't it be a waste to put the corpse in the bin?

As I stared at the chicken, considering my options, the pesto-flavoured meal began to stir. It wasn't the first time a cockroach had found a home in my fridge, but I was no less disturbed. I poked at the chicken, hoping to scare the roach away. But as my finger sunk into the pesto sauce, I realised this was no roach.

It was a handsome auburn feather.

It wiggled on its own, repelling the green sauce as it rose to the surface. I stopped breathing, my armpits slick with sweat.

Another feather rose. And another.

The sauce started to bubble, pieces of days-old chicken frothing at the surface, spilling to the ground with a dreadful *splat*. I threw the dish across the room, screaming in tandem with the crash of glass as a framed photo of me and my ex-boyfriend fell to the floor.

The green pesto continued to froth and boil, steam rising. More feathers leaked from the sauce as I approached the hot mess. Broken glass lay across the floor, melting into the sauce, the photo untouched.

I knelt and picked it up, ignoring the rush of regret for how my ex and I had left things: messy. In the picture, we stood in our snow gear, arms wrapped around each other's shoulders, smiles beaming at the camera. Perisher Blue: our first weekend getaway as a couple.

As I reminisced, the photo began to burn at the edges as if someone held a lighter underneath. My eyes, captured in that moment of happiness, felt scratched. The menacing cluck returned, taunting me with its rage.

Scratching my eyes out.

It was a warning, I knew. If I didn't act now, make up for what I'd done, the chicken would come for my eyes. And who knew what else?

I placed the photo down, taking short, sharp breaths. The pesto sauce beneath me looked more like bubbling tar now – black, thick, steaming. The feathers continued to force their way out, rising into the air as if carried on a phantom breeze. The same breeze my victim had felt. The last thing he'd felt before I tore his life away.

"I'm so sorry," I whispered towards the sauce. It bubbled and gurgled in response. Had it heard me?

From the black mess on the floor came that clucking again. The high-pitched noise screeched through my brain. I covered my ears and fell to the floor, my face an inch away from the black pesto tar. Something wet leaked from my ears.

"I'm sorry!" I cried.

The bubbling liquid reached my face – a beak opening wide. Peckish. Starving. It wanted my blood. I fell backwards, avoiding its grasp, crawling away on my backside. I ignored the squishy feeling in my underwear and the stench of my last meal.

I pressed myself against a wall. With nowhere left to go, I was helpless to evade the tar as it continued to take shape. As it made its way towards me, the form was clear. Of course, it was clear. There was nothing else it could be.

Brrrrrrrkk.

The chicken came towards me. I raised my hands to my face, screaming for forgiveness. I tasted tears and sweat and wished the fiendish creature would leave me alone. Drops of tar fell from its body, hissing against the floorboards. The chicken cocked its head towards me, pecking at my legs and feet. The pecks left burn marks on my skin.

Climbing on top of me, the chicken spread its tar feathers wide. It released another high-pitched cluck. My ears bled once more, and just when I thought my head would burst –

The chicken exploded in front of me.

A mess of tar and feathers drenched my apartment, my body covered in the hot liquid. At least the chicken was gone. For now.

The tar burned against my skin. I ran to the bathroom. Despite the apartment only being a few years old, the pipes had always been a little unpredictable. The shower worked, but it was anyone's guess as to whether the water would heat up. The bath was much more reliable. In my haste to remove the hot liquid from my body, I bypassed the shower and ran myself a warm bath.

The water gushed into the tub, flowing around my ankles. I was conscious that my bare arse reeked of my accidental pooping, and I wiped the mess with some toilet paper. The resulting stain was auburn, and I couldn't help but shudder. It felt like the chicken was inside me, scratching away from somewhere in my core.

I sat down in the bath, letting the warm water absorb into my skin. Thankfully, I always kept some bubble bath on standby for unwinding after those stressful days in the office. I poured a generous amount near the tap's stream. The white, foamy bubbles stood in contrast to the tarry pesto bubbling a moment ago, but my heart still beat faster.

It's okay, I thought, breathing from my lower chakras. *The spirit is gone.*

Twisting the tap off, I settled into the tub. My knees, exposed above the water line, made me think of little mountains rising from the ocean. As I washed the gunk from my face and arms, the tar sank to the bottom of the bath, hidden by the purity of the white bubbles forming islands across the surface. Once my face was clean, I took a few deep breaths and rested my eyes.

This haunting stuff was exhausting. I felt like I hadn't had a proper sleep for days, though the incident at the farm had only been yesterday. The irony of all this was that I hadn't even wanted to go. Since my parents had passed – one after the other – Uncle John was all I had left. He was a career farmer and didn't have time for love, so there were no cousins or even distant relatives.

Before the cancer took her, my mum had whispered to me to look after poor old Uncle John. I sensed that she'd said the same thing to him about me, to make sure we kept together whatever remnants of the family survived.

I thought about Uncle John as the bubbles began their soft popping. Had he ever been haunted by the thousands of chickens he'd murdered? I gathered that otherwise, he'd have found a new career quickly. If this was only happening to me, the question was: why?

Wrapped in my thoughts and comforted by the warm water caressing my skin, I almost failed to notice a deep red chicken comb slicing through the water between my legs. Inching closer to my nether regions.

Something sharp brushed against my shrinking gonads.

I opened my eyes and slid backwards in the tub, splashing bubbles and water through the bathroom. The chicken comb stabbed towards me, five blades ready to slice me open. I kicked at the blades and fought them off with my hands, drawing blood from each finger.

Brrrrrrrkk.

The chicken rose from the water, its tiny eyes wide

with rage. I held its head back as it pecked and clawed beneath the water. The possibility of being admired at the bathhouse was in real danger. My inner thighs burned as the chicken dug its claws and beak into my meaty flesh. Pecking me apart.

I climbed out of the bath, pulling the plug chain with my foot as I hit the wet tiles. The bubbles and the water and the blood from my fingers circled down the drain, clogged for a moment by the tar. I punched and squealed as the chicken clung to my inner thigh, its claws flexing beneath my skin.

As the drain unclogged itself, clumps of tar spinning into the pipes, the maniacal chicken clucked and clawed. The waterborne monster fought the current but was getting sucked down the hole with everything else. I punched again, landing a fist in the chicken's face. It unclenched from my thigh, clucking as it was sucked into the drain.

The final slurp of the chicken disappearing from the tub left me both hopeful and terrified.

It had had every intention of removing my body parts. I held a hand against the wound in my thigh and checked my groin for any damage. The shrivelled little soldier had made it out unscathed, my future children safe for now.

Sensing that I didn't have long until the chicken returned, I bandaged my thigh, pulled on some clothes, and let the front door slam behind me as I limped towards the local vegan market. I needed help.

Book of Shaman:
"The Massacre at Roanoke" Part Two
Roanoke, North America, 1585

"THE HEART IS THE BEST part."

Mack had picked the hearts out of the pile of guts and organs that James had thrown away. Before James could protest, he had dropped them into the pot. The man dipped a grimy pinky into the broth and tasted it. A smile spread across his face.

Mack smacked James on the back again, this time with affection. "Good stew, mate."

He left James to stare into the gurgling water, the hearts sinking to the bottom.

The carcasses floated through the water, the meat tenderising with each bubble farting to the surface. James added turnips, potatoes, and other root vegetables to the stew, twisting a wooden ladle around the pot in circles. He shed a tear when a raccoon heart bobbed to the surface.

Never kill again. Never kill again.

Stirring the stew, James remembered the raccoon

fiddling in the grass, going about its business. Now, its hide would end up as a hat. James sneered at the trend of wearing animal parts as accessories. He couldn't see it lasting. How many raccoons would it take to make a fur coat, anyway?

How would they like their skin to be paraded around as a hat?

The thought seeped out of his brain and into the air around him before floating towards the pile of bones at the back of the cooking area. The power of thought had been theorized for some time by philosophers everywhere, but their ideas had yet to reach James or the other colonists.

As James' rage and hurt and guilt filled the air in the kitchen, erasing the scent of the broth of the murder victims, the power of thought began to twist into something tangible.

The air thickened around him. Sound vanished. The bubbling of the water, gone. No wind, no birds cawing, no children laughing. Just the heat of the air and the sound of the raccoon hearts.

Thump-thump. Thump-thump. Thump-thump.

He stared at the hearts, expanding and contracting with a life force stolen only hours earlier. His hearing rushed back, an explosion in his eardrums. He fell to the ground as bloodcurdling screams echoed through the village.

Making his way to the kitchen door and pushing through to the outside, James ignored the light glowing from the pile of dead raccoons. There was no time to think about that now.

Instead, he saw the colonists. His friends. His neighbours. Parents scrambling with children in their arms, tears streaming across blood-drenched faces. Others cowered under tables as sailors took up arms with their muskets, shooting into the night without knowing where to aim.

He saw shadows shaped like animals. Opaque apparitions. Raccoons.

Have I done this? Did my guilt give life to their souls?

He saw sharp teeth shred through Mrs Wordsworth, the wife of one of the men in the hunting party. Her throat torn out, splatting into the dirt metres from where she lay. She clutched at the gash for a moment before going limp. A shadow moved on to the next colonist.

The source of Mrs Wordsworth's injuries became less opaque with each bite of flesh. The raccoons discarded skin and fragments of bone the way the hunting party had done to them. This was their revenge. James stared at the scene, unmoving. Unable to feel anger towards the spirits.

Governor Lane emerged from his tent and ran into the action wearing a shirt and no pants. His member flopped about amidst his hurried motions through the crowd. Confusion captured his face. The governor pointed his pistol here and there, clearly afraid to shoot a colonist by mistake.

James saw a raccoon behind him and shouted to the governor to hide. But the raccoon pounced as Governor Ralph Lane twisted around, his short member shrinking like a turtle head.

James covered his eyes, and when he opened them, the governor was nothing more than a pile of chunky red flesh and a tiny flaccid penis.

The governor's mistress emerged from the tent a moment later, fixing a wig and pulling drawers over a thick piece of anatomy that ought not to have been there. The worst-kept secret in the colony squealed, slipping on the wilting flesh. Before his bottom hit ground, the mistress' neck was gripped in the jaw of another raccoon. Maybe the same one that had killed the governor.

Children screamed, drawing James away from the scene. They pointed, and James saw another raccoon under the yellow glow of the moon.

No, he thought and counted. Seventeen raccoons.

James reached for a knife – the knife he'd used to skin the raccoons – and gripped the handle. A group of children he'd often kicked a ball around with were huddled against a tree, watching their parents and neighbours fall prey to the vengeful ghosts of the native wildlife.

He raced through the battle zone, tripping over a stray arm here and slipping over a string of intestines there. He almost fell atop a colon. He kicked aside a hand, its finger still on the trigger of a fallen musket,

Over the screams and chaos, Mack called to James and joined him in the effort to reach the cowering children. He was missing an eye, and half his face looked mauled, yet somehow the man still lived. He threw a weapon to James, who let it hit the ground with a thud. Mack started to yell at him but knew there was no time. No time to yell, no time to go and pick up the gun. They rushed towards the children, calling to them with assurances that they would be alright.

Even to James, as uneducated as he was, this sounded stupid. They were not going to be alright. None of them were. The raccoons tore limb from body and head from shoulders with an ease nobody had seen before.

They reached the tree, and a young girl squeezed James' neck in a terrified embrace. For a moment, James felt hope. That maybe this was a horrible nightmare, or they'd been poisoned with some strange native plant. But as the young girl gripped tighter, choking the air from his lungs, James saw the glowing eyes blinking at him from beyond the tree line.

Teeth bared like jagged knives. It was as though the animal smiled at him, revelling in its power. Over him. Over them all.

"Please," James whispered, hoarse and desperate. "Not the children."

A second pair of eyes glowed through the dim light. A third.

The children squealed as the eyes circled them.

Four pairs.

Five.

More raccoons joined them, encircling the group of frightened children. It was then that James realised that aside from their own heavy breaths, there was no other sound.

No more screams or muskets shooting into the air.

Nothing.

James lost count of the eyes, wielding the knife towards the spirits as he ushered the children behind him. He pried the girl from his neck, sucked in a deep breath, and waved the knife at their enemies again.

"Take me," James begged. "Leave the children alone."

With nothing but a kitchen knife to protect himself and the children, he knew it was over. These creatures, these apparitions, weren't afraid of a knife. They were beyond the physical realm.

"These children are innocents," Mack agreed, gun poised at his waist. "Whatever your quarrel, it is not with them."

Whatever their quarrel? James thought. *We slaughtered them!*

The raccoons glared at the men, then at James, seeming to read his thoughts. Understanding his guilt and shame. Understanding that of the two men, only one felt anything – perhaps remorse – for their actions. The other still wore a hat made from the skin of their fallen brother.

James saw Mack squeeze his finger around the trigger at his waist and called for Mack to stop. The man should have known it would be useless, but he squeezed a second time, aiming at the raccoon in front of him.

The animals seemed to laugh at him, cackling into the night sky in sordid glee. James fell to his knees, knife in hand, and pleaded for forgiveness. His words echoed through the colony, silenced by another bullet whizzing towards the raccoons.

"Do not beg these monsters," Mack spat at James. "They are our enemy."

Shaking his head, James muttered that Mack didn't understand. Pulled at his shirt. But he shot again. Each of the bullets missed, of course. There was nothing to hit. The raccoons were just spirits awoken by vengeance.

They moved closer, circling Mack, who adopted an offensive posture. Fists raised as if they would hit anything. James pulled at his shirt again and begged him to stop, but Mack thrust him away.

"I will defend this colony," he said through gritted teeth.

"The colony is gone," James shouted back. "Look around! It's all gone!"

The raccoons inched closer still, a breath away from Mack's legs, ready to attack. As Mack punched forward, hitting only air, the raccoons hissed in delight and pounced.

James raced to cover the children's eyes as the raccoons tore through Mack's flesh. Their claws dug into the man, begging now when it was too late. They scratched at his skin, severed nerves, and made a mess of his tendon and muscle. Mack's screams dwindled and faded as his life spewed into the dirt around him.

James caught sight of a beating heart, exposed to the cool night air before the beasts threw it into the woods like refuse. When the carcass was nothing more than shreds of flesh and bone, the raccoons turned to James and the children.

James whispered, "I'm sorry."

The raccoons glared at the knife, still in his hands, shaking and sweaty. James released his grip. The knife clattered against the ground, the raccoons' eyes fixed on the metal object. They stepped back, gnashing their teeth.

One raccoon stepped forward. Met James' eyes. Held his gaze. It saw into his soul. Saw his regret. Made him vow on his life and the lives of the children that he would never kill again. In the following moments, he knew this land was not theirs.

The raccoon spoke to him in hisses and growls and yowls. This land had never been for man. It would never be theirs. *Leave this place. Or pay the price to stay.*

James nodded his agreement. They would leave. An unspoken deal had been struck.

The raccoons began to fade into nothingness until only one remained, still holding James' gaze. It bared its teeth again and vanished.

An overwhelming quiet met the group, huddling alone in the night amidst the stench of the gore. James herded the children together as buzzards were drawn to the mess like bees to nectar. They abandoned the village, leaving the broth to boil, the clothes to dry, the fire to burn out.

As they neared the surf, James spotted a tree, its bark scratched. A single word. Croatoan.

He only understood it to mean, *Never kill again*.

PART II

JAMES WAVED GOODBYE TO THE Lawrence family, watching Mr Lawrence disperse pastries to the children just outside the door. At the same time, Mrs Lawrence fidgeted with an umbrella for the dreary British weather. The children danced about in excited glee, with a moment of sibling rivalry at the girl being given the larger pie. James smiled to himself, cherishing the exchange.

Since his return to England some years ago, life has been good to him. The old bakery on Fleet Street had been empty when the ship had pulled into the docks, and he'd picked up where he left off, those three words always echoing in the back of his mind.

Never kill again.

And he hadn't.

His supply for the meat pies came from the local butcher, a friendly old chap by the name of Riggs. The meat came prepared and ready to go, without the fear of retribution from any old enemies.

Riggs' daughter was something to behold. At first sight, James thought he'd died and gone to heaven, as clichéd as that seemed. Her face struck him like a thousand blows – the beauty too much to bear. Golden hair framed her pale face. Deep emerald eyes stared straight through him. Uncovered every dark secret, each of his deepest desires. She could have them. She could have anything she wanted.

His return to England saw business grow steady and his knees grow weak. Pearl Riggs took a liking to him, flitting her eyelashes as they exchanged secret smiles. The romance was fast and intense, with her growing belly soon ushering wedding bells and the shrieks of a newborn.

Mackenzie James White was born on the fourth day of the fourth month. His features resembled those of his mother, a mercy for which James thanked the heavens each and every day.

As life went on, the horrors of Roanoke sank further to the back of his mind, only emerging at strange moments, often without reason.

When Mackenzie clapped at a butterfly.

When Mackenzie stamped at a cockroach.

When Mackenzie, now four years old, said he wanted to go fishing with Pearl's father, James put his foot down.

"I will not have you participating in that barbarism," he said, wagging a finger in the boy's face.

The child had stormed to Pearl, crashing into her bosom with tears and sorrow and mumbling about how unfair life was for children these days. How monstrous his father was. Those poor fish swimming all alone in the river with nobody to catch them.

Mackenzie went on and on, as four-year-olds were want to do. But James did not relent. Pearl's eyes begged him to change his mind – after all, other boys did such things, and their baby boy already suffered from awkwardness around his peers.

As the day dwindled into night, and James closed the shop, he took a deep breath and headed upstairs, where he and his beloved family resided – the time had come to share his past. His role in the Roanoke massacre.

Lighting a candle by the bed and slipping under the covers with his wife, James recounted his story.

"What happened to the children?" she whispered.

"We started to swim to a neighbouring island. One of the children started to drown. I held his head above the water. I didn't know how long I could keep it up. I could feel myself sinking into the ocean when a fisherman caught sight of us and pulled us into his boat. A kind old man. He rescued us."

"Oh, James." Pearl pressed a hand over her heart. "How horrible."

James looked into those emerald eyes and smiled. He caressed her hand and kissed her soft skin.

"I stayed at the island for some time until finally, another colony ship arrived. I convinced the captain to bring me back to London, bartering my cooking skills for safe passage."

They talked into the night until their bedside candle burned out. He slept well in the knowledge that his sordid past was now known and that his wife still cherished him. Everything would be alright, just as he'd said to the children all those years ago.

James awoke the following morning as the roosters sang to the rising sun. His favourite time of the day, when everyone else was sleeping, and he could whistle a tune or two as he set up the shop for another day of bread, pies, and assorted pastries.

But the roosters were not the only thing he heard that morning. A disturbing sound underneath the floorboards. In the walls.

Scratching.

James jumped out of bed and pressed his ear to the wall to hear a sound familiar to London's working class – the creatures from the dark. Creatures that traded on death and left behind sickness. Rats.

If the rats got to the meat below, the bakery would have to shut its doors. No baking meant no money. No money meant – well, no nothing. With this knowledge in mind, James ran downstairs, eyes peeled for any sight of the vermin. He grabbed a knife, intending to destroy the rats any way he could –

Never kill again.

He dropped the knife to grab a broom, intending to sweep the critters out the front door. Let someone else handle them. Then he saw it.

A long tail, like a strand of twine moving of its own accord. James approached the creature, its body not yet visible. Just the tail snaking along the floor, leaving a trail in the dust. He saw tiny, clawed footprints leading to the pantry.

Never kill again.

Swallowing his rage, James rushed to the pantry, pulled the door open, and stomped his feet as a warning. The rat sat in the corner, gnawing at a fallen chunk of cheese. The broom's bristles brushed the floor as James swept towards the creature. The rat slowly turned its head, its eyes, black and empty, glared at the baker and its expression seemed almost indignant. 'How dare you?'

"Please," James said, "just leave me alone."

The rat bared its teeth, just like the raccoons all those years ago, and stood up on its back legs, hissing. James screamed, fell backwards, and the broom landed atop of him. Before he could stand, the rat rushed towards him, hissing and spitting as vermin were known to do. It crawled onto his leg, tiny claws digging into the skin of his calves.

James begged again. His cries were pointless.

The rat continued up his body, towards his neck and face. Its empty eyes told him that his flesh was better than a stinky piece of cheese.

James squeezed his hands around the rat, but the creature squirmed and slipped through his grip. A monster that could stretch itself to unnatural lengths. Squeeze through tiny holes.

The rat landed on James' face, nuzzled its pointy nose into his neck, and bit.

Tore his flesh apart and burrowed into his body.

James grabbed the rat's tail, pulled it from his neck, and threw it against the pantry wall. His vision was blurred, his wound gushing like the edge of a waterfall. Holding a hand to his neck, James crawled towards the blood-soaked rat, lying motionless from the impact against the wall.

As the blood pooled around both of them, James clenched his hand into a fist and thrust it down on the rat's body. The squish was satisfying, and he went for seconds, pummelling the rat until its innards were as minced as one of his pies.

Never kill again.

With his last breaths, James wept. He had broken his promise and killed an animal. As his life faded, the uncertainty of what his actions would mean for his family haunted him.

"What have I done?" he choked into the empty room.

Soon, the rat and James White were dead.

HER SON'S SCREAMS WOKE PEARL, who hastened down the staircase to the bakery below.

The boy stood by the pantry, howling for his father to wake up. As Pearl approached the scene, she gasped and rushed through the sheen of her husband's blood to take her son outside. Pearl slammed the bakery door shut and almost slipping on the cobbled road, all the while hollering with all her might for help. For a constable. For anyone.

Some kind of accident, the police said, who took his body and offered to clean up the mess, but Pearl just sat by the door with her son, refusing to cross the threshold. In her almost catatonic condition – and, of course, being a woman in 1592 – decisions for her future were left to the men around her. Mr Riggs and his brother – known by most, for some reason, as Uncle Riggs – decided a fresh start in America would help Pearl gain some distance from the horrors of Fleet Street.

As Pearl and Mackenzie were led towards the harbour, luggage in tow and hearts in their throats, Mr Riggs welcomed the new tenant to the bakery. Someone named Lovett. Pearl couldn't put her finger on it, but something told her that the bakery would someday have its own sordid history.

And so it was that Pearl and Mackenzie White accompanied Uncle Riggs to America.

FOUR

THE VEGAN MARKET WAS A few blocks from my apartment building, but it might as well have been a different planet. I didn't want to admit it, but these vegan characters were in a league of their own. Not all of them, of course, but the evidence before me as I entered the market indicated that a large majority were either current or ex-hippies.

"Hey, bro," a guy in his mid-fifties greeted me. I was sure his thick, wiry hair had swallowed many a comb. His eyebrows loomed large, too.

"Um." I cleared my throat. "Sup?"

The guy nodded in response, as though my hippy jargon had made perfect sense, and spread his arms wide. "Welcome to Vegan H(e)aven, bro. How can I help you in an ecologically responsible way?"

I arched an eyebrow and looked sideways, unsure how to engage with this creature. It almost made the chicken haunting seem manageable. But I did have a serious problem, and all the Reddit threads had suggested turning to veganism, so I had no choice but to engage.

"I'm new to this vegan stuff." I shrugged. "Is there, like, a starter pack or something?"

The shop worker – *Jethro* according to his name tag –

squinted into the distance, nodding and smiling like he was talking to something on his shoulder. He gave the occasional "Yeah, man" and "That's sweet", along with a snicker here and there.

"Hello?" I waved a hand in front of his face. "No pressure – uh, bro – but it's kind of urgent."

Jethro returned to the present. "Urgent, huh?"

I leaned in and whispered, "Maybe even life and death."

Veganism was always about life and death. The lives of those poor little chickens and whatever other animals mattered these days always hung in the balance. I was just starting to appreciate the complexities of taking a life, yet to Jethro, it somehow seemed old hat.

He sized me up, then his eyes wandered the store's shelves. After a few moments, he leaned an elbow against the counter and smirked.

"I can *definitely* do you a starter pack," he said, "but it won't be cheap."

The word "cheap" echoed in my brain. *Cheep-cheep* – like a cluster of baby chicks calling for their lost brethren. I shook it off and told Jethro that money was no object.

He raced around the shop, pulling faux bacon, chicken-less breasts, cow-inspired patties, and nut-based cheese from the shelves. I almost saw the dollar signs in his eyes as he filled a shopping cart, taking two of everything – because, as he told me with glee, you can't stop at just one.

As Jethro threw half the store into a trolley with my name on it, I was distracted by a community noticeboard. The local vegan community, if that was a real thing, had lots to share, it seemed: a vegan cake fair, a charity event for plant-based medical supplies, a rally in the name of Bobby the Bull, who had succumbed to the violence of being a primary school's football mascot. I was about to turn away and pay for my new diet when I noticed an advertisement.

Vegan Shaman and Demonologist, the ad read. *Exorcising all your animal-based demons. From burial ceremonies to possession, Vegan Shaman has you covered! Call now for a free quote and help a poor, tortured animal move on.*

A vegan shaman? I shook my head in disbelief. *Sounds like a basket* case.

Nonetheless, I tore a strip of paper containing the shaman's phone number from the bottom of the advert.

"He's quite good," Jethro said over my shoulder. His breath stunk of beans and tomato-based sauces.

"Sounds like a scam artist," I said, folding the paper into my pocket.

Jethro shook his head. "Oh, no," he said. "He's helped lots of people. Last year, a twelve-year-old girl was possessed by the unhappy soul of her guinea pig. He fixed her right up. And just last week, he proved that Mr Morley was not guilty of murder because he was possessed by a raven. His body pecked out all those eyes, but dude, the authorities refused to believe the raven's spirit committed the crime."

"So, what happened to Mr Morley?"

"That's not important, really." Jethro waved the question out of existence. "You should hire him if you have some kind of trouble."

I left the store with three hundred dollars' worth of cardboard food and a new appreciation of shamanism.

I texted the number – 1800 SHAMAN – and hoped my problem would be solved.

My name is Harry Peck. Being haunted by a chicken. Please help me, my text read.

The response was immediate, my phone buzzing in my hand. I fumbled with my bags, dropping some imitation ham to the concrete below. The local pigeons weren't even tempted, and neither were the stray cats. This revelation first made me question how my stomach would cope with the sudden change in my diet. As I read the shaman's reply, I put that thought to the side.

This is more common than people think. Vegan Shaman can help you!

I found it odd that the shaman referred to himself in the third person, but my desperation enabled me to look the other way. We texted back and forth for a few minutes, the groceries getting heavier in my arms as I awaited confirmation from Vegan Shaman that he could come to my apartment as soon as possible. I relayed the seriousness of the situation and the malevolence of the entity trying to destroy me. Again, Vegan Shaman assured me he could help.

Fear not, the final message said. *Vegan Shaman will be at your apartment within the hour!*

Slipping my phone into my jeans pocket, I found renewed strength. I left the imitation ham on the road for whatever animal dared to play chicken with it, so to speak. Rushing through the city, the shadow of a chicken following close behind, I was back at my apartment in just under fifteen minutes.

I found myself standing outside the door, fingers paused at the handle. I ignored the pained clucking sound the rusty hinges made as I pushed the door open, certain it was my imagination twisting the noise into something that wasn't there.

The absence of sound in the apartment was eerie. The washing machine still beeped, and I heard the subtle tick of my owl-shaped wall clock, but a strange stillness hung in the air. I had that feeling you get when you're hiding in the closet, waiting to scare someone. The anticipation and excitement coalesced into a thick silence.

I dropped the bags in the kitchen and started unpacking the variety of vegan products Jethro had deemed necessary. He'd been thorough, including vegan chocolate for those sweet cravings and vegan flour, whatever that even meant. Without much regard, I stocked the shelves, checking my watch now and then.

Come on, Vegan Shaman.

As I pulled mushroom burger patties from the bag and threw them in the fridge with a grimace, I heard the distinct sound of static.

The television had come on in the living room by itself. Despite being a smart TV, it had somehow found an unused channel. Black-and-white snow filled the screen.

"No, no…" I shook my head. "Not now!"

I moved to the living room. The TV blared with static, drowning out the beeping washing machine and the wall clock. It was almost as if time itself had stopped, holding me hostage. I couldn't look away.

I dropped to my knees and searched for the remote. It

was hidden beneath the couch, though I couldn't figure out how it had gotten there. I reached for it, dodging old lolly wrappers and balls of fluff from God knew what.

The static grew louder as my fingers clutched the remote. I stabbed the OFF button, digging my nail into the rubber when it did nothing. Stabbed again and again. Slapped the remote against my knee to jog the batteries awake. Tried again, with no result.

A form began to emerge in the blacks, whites, and greys of the static.

Brrrrrrrkk.

"Please stop," I begged. "I'm a vegan now!"

The chicken seeped from the screen, its beak and wings melting through the glass. Its black eyes glared at me as it pulled itself from the television, a physical form birthed from the static.

I ran to the kitchen, grabbed a chicken-less breast, and laid it in front of the staticky demon as an offering for my crime.

"Take it," I cried. "Take it!"

The chicken ignored my peace offering and crept closer, dragging its thick backside out of the television and into my reality. The tips of its wings were no longer auburn feathers. The static had mutated them into something else. They were made of exposed bone, scraping along the floorboards as it approached me.

Brrrrrrrkk, the chicken cried, pulling free one leg, then another. Its head pecked back and forth in search of something.

At that moment, with the demon chicken pecking towards me, I gave up. The fight was over. I'd shot it in cold blood, and this was its revenge. I deserved to die, and if my death would bring peace to this poor lost soul, then so be it.

I took a deep breath as I embraced my fate. "It's okay," I said, encouraging the chicken towards me. "Do what you must —"

"Be gone, beast of the devil!"

I turned to see an older man at the front door. He wore a thick overcoat and a wide-brimmed hat. Salt-and-pepper hair framed his face and adorned his chin. His brown eyes seemed to dare the chicken to make another move.

"I said *be gone!*" he repeated, pointing a thick forefinger at the creature. He wore a dark emerald ring, and it glowed in the sunlight.

The chicken clucked and clawed but did not move further into the room. It glared at the man and spread its wings. I knew this move. Bracing for the tar explosion, I shut my eyes and readied myself.

I heard the man's heavy footsteps as he raced into the living room, reciting something in Latin. The chicken screeched. He repeated the Latin phrase, and I opened my eyes to watch the master at work.

Cowering before him, the chicken let out a final painful cry before evaporating like a shadow in the strength of the sun.

Heavy breathing filled the apartment for a few seconds as the man composed himself, and I searched for traces of the chicken. We were alone, this man and me, and I found myself worrying about my bowel movements.

No smell, no dark stains on my jeans. *Third time's the charm*, I thought, and smiled.

The man held his hand out to me. I took it and thanked him for his help.

"You have one angry chicken on your hands," he said. "But first, let me introduce myself. I am Vegan Shaman."

Book of Shaman:
"The Otter of Sioux Falls"
Village of Sioux Falls, South Dakota, 1880

THE VILLAGE AT SIOUX FALLS had become permanent only a few years ago, after some fifty years of explorers and settlements traipsing through the land. Margaret Weiss read the pamphlet literature on the carriage ride to her new home. As was often the case with families of lower socioeconomic status, Margaret had been sold off for marriage to an irrigation engineer at the village. Her father had brokered the deal despite Margaret's tears and protests. He wrapped his arms around her, hushed her through soothing whispers, and assured her that the family needed the money. It was either trade the last two milk-producing goats or sell his beloved daughter.

How could she argue? She was no match for the goats.

Margaret was of child-bearing age and had been told she had the hips for it – whatever that meant – so the choice, to her father, was obvious. Margaret admitted it was the most viable option for the success of her family but couldn't shake the feeling that she was nothing more than a vessel to be shipped around by the will of the men in her life.

Her new husband, Gregory Cox, was the village's lead engineer. From what she'd been told, his family had a long history across continents. An ancestor of his, Mackenzie White, had been a famous writer of what had come to be known as "penny dreadfuls," regaling readers everywhere with tales of flesh-eating apparitions and ferocious rats. Margaret had read a few of the works but could not stomach the descriptions' raw intensity.

As the horse-drawn carriage rocked to and fro along the Sioux River, which glimmered in the summer heat, Margaret hoped her new owner – husband – was at least handsome and kind.

She'd been purchased sight unseen, which was more common than Margaret would have liked. How would either of them know they would be happy with the purchase? He might want a thin blonde, rather than a plumpish thing with freckles and dark hair. It was too late now, though. She was almost there.

Gregory Cox was indeed a charming man. He was rugged but in a boyish way. He had a nervous smile and a twinkle in his eye as he helped Margaret down from the carriage. His hands were rough, as an engineer's should be, but his attention to her was soft and warm.

"Hello, Miss Margaret." Gregory's voice was almost inaudible.

She smiled back, butterflies wreaking havoc in her stomach. "Hello."

And so she came to be known as Miss Margaret, even after

their wedding that night. She would grow to call him Coxhead when she was mad at him, and Mr C when she was not.

As the heat melted away and the leaves grew brown and red, Gregory trudged into the house, kissed Margaret on the forehead, and slumped at the dining table. Margaret rubbed her belly, taking a deep breath as the baby kicked again.

"How was your day, Mr C?" Margaret asked, hoping to distract herself from the jabbing in her gut.

"Another river otter caught in the system today." He wiped the sweat from his brow and sighed. "Those bloody animals don't know what's good for them."

"What does it mean for the village water supply?" Margaret asked.

Gregory shook his head and stared at his sore feet. "It means we lost another pump. The poor animal was squashed to death in there. The water is full of blood. It's no good."

Margaret contemplated for a moment, still rubbing circles on her belly. "Why don't you just kill them all?"

Gregory looked at his wife blankly. "What do you mean?"

She shrugged. "Well, if they are ruining the village water supply, they should be removed from the equation."

"Equation? Miss Margaret!" Gregory exasperatedly slammed a fist on the table. "These are living creatures!"

"And? The villagers kill animals all the time. For food, for clothing. Damnation, even Mr Rathbone skinned that cow for a nice rug the other week. Remember that, Mr C?"

Gregory nodded.

"Remember how beautiful that rug was?" Margaret pushed. "I hope our son will have nice things like that someday."

"There won't be anything nice if I don't fix this problem." Gregory fell into silence and then slapped the table again. "If only there was some way to reroute them from the river."

"There is," Margaret said. When Gregory widened his eyes in anticipation, urging her to put her brilliant idea into words, she continued, "Kill them."

Gregory sighed and kissed his wife on the forehead as he walked toward the front door.

"I'm going to have a lager with the boys."

He had always been taught to appreciate and respect animals. His father and grandfather instilled in him the belief that animals were precious. Sure, they were used as food for our nourishment – but let someone else do the killing.

Kill them.

As he remembered his father's lessons, Margaret's words rattled through his brain. Listening to the owls hoot at the moon, those nights by the campfire. Those days in the fields, watching cows moo and lift their tails to piss anywhere they wanted. Things were simple then.

But now, Margaret's words were striking a chord. The village depended on him for water. He was the head engineer, after all. He and his team had tried netting; they'd built a wall to stop the otters from reaching too far down the river. Neither had worked. The poor creatures got stuck in the net and simply jumped the wall. It was almost like they were attracted to the irrigation system, swimming straight to it like a moth to a flame.

Sucking down his lager, Gregory told his friends about his wife's idea, expecting outcries of shame and horror. His four companions just sat there, eyeing each other in silence.

"It's not the way," Gregory said and took another swig.

"To be fair," Charlie Mansen said, "it's not *without* merit."

Nods from the other three around the table. Charlie took this as a measure of support and continued.

"We have *tried* to do the right thing here, Gregory." His voice was low but firm.

"There is only so much time we can waste on this. The best thing to do here is remove them from the equation."

"Suddenly, everyone is a mathematics expert," Gregory muttered.

He zoned out as the boys chattered away. He heard words here and there – *spikes, spears, poison* – but contributed nothing. Just sucked away at his lager until he found himself scooping out froth from the sides of the glass.

"It's settled, then." Charlie raised his glass for a toast. Gregory did not join in. "The otters die at sunrise."

The following day was a blur of blood and the yelping of otters as they were speared through their tiny hearts and brains. Gregory, to his everlasting shame, participated in the slaughter. Voices in the back of his mind told him to stop, to drop his spear, and go straight home to his wife and unborn child. Yet he did not. He took up arms with his colleagues and peers, stood in the river like a fisherman stalking trout.

Felt the water rush past his bare ankles. Felt the burn in his chest for the impending sin.

Felt the pressure of his spear as it pierced an otter's skin.

The force of the wood pummelled through its body and stabbed into the wet earth. Its eyes glazed over after a few moments of fishtailing and gagging on its own blood. The red washed away with the river's, but the body remained.

Among the gleeful "huzzahs" of his colleagues, Gregory thought he saw a white glow around the otter's body – just for a second, maybe less – not long enough to be sure he'd seen anything at all. But his heart had seen inside itself, had seen the evil of which he was capable.

Ripping the spear out of the otter's corpse, he threw it into the river and tore at his hair. Collapsing into the water, Gregory wept for the otter he'd killed. For all the otters dying around him.

THE NIGHT WAS COLD, AND Gregory sat by the fire, unable to stop trembling. The orange glow cast half his face in darkness as he stared into the depths of the fire. Wood crackled and smoke rose, stinging his eyes. Margaret fussed about behind him, mumbling that he was too close to the heat, nagging at him to move away.

But Gregory was freezing. His fingers were purple from the cold, despite holding them over the flames. Margaret stood behind him and rubbed her warm hands over his bare arms.

"We'll get you warm in no time," she whispered into the fire.

Gregory knew her eff orts were in vain, for it wasn't the bite in the air that kept his skin like a plucked goose. It was his guilt.

After what felt like hours of Margaret's kind attempts to warm him, she settled into bed, singing to the baby in her belly. Gregory sat by the flames, watching the shapes and shadows that moved about on the wall. Shapes that twisted into otters. Shadows that grew across the wall, hovering above him. In the dim light, the shadows seemed to stretch from the confines of the wall into the room itself. Gregory wiped tears from his eyes and sniffled into the silence, sure that his guilt was playing tricks on him.

Until the high-pitched whimpering came from flames. Gregory sat back in his chair, trembling in a cold sweat, and watched the shadows march across the room. The whimpering persisted into the night, though Margaret did not stir. It was as though the noise was meant just for him.

The shadows emerged from the wall, mewling like a creature in pain. Taking the shape of an otter. The poor creature he'd murdered earlier that day. Its fur was brown but misshapen, matted and wet like dead grass melting into the earth. Gregory stared into the creature's eyes as it pulled itself from the shadow realm into his reality. His fear and guilt kept him from running or screaming or doing anything at all.

The creature came towards him, fully formed now, trailing embers and wailing into the flame-lit room. It pounced onto Gregory's lap and sniffed at his neck and face. Even now, as the creature dominated him, Gregory could not move. He trembled and shook, but those were involuntary movements from the biting cold that would not go away.

Gregory took a sharp breath, before convulsing as the creature dug at his chest, seeking his heart. But the spirit's nails didn't tear or burn his flesh. No, it's touch chilled his blood, turning it into rivers blocked by ice floes. His chest crackled as ice formed under the skin.

As the cold took him and the otter squirmed around inside him, Gregory uttered a silent prayer for his unborn child. The child must not make the same mistake.

And as the fire crackled into nothingness, he knew that this was his penance for taking a life. He'd known his fate was that his life would be cut short because of his actions, but he had only hoped to see his new child before he was taken. Now it was too late. A child unseen. A story untold. That was the real penance. The tragedy of their family history was to be lost.

WHEN MARGARET AWOKE THE FOLLOWING morning, Gregory sat unmoving on the couch. She laid a hand on his shoulder and recoiled at the frost. "Mr C?" she asked, voice low and soft.

His eyes did not blink. His chest did not rise and fall. He was covered in a layer of ice, bitten by a frost that had no reason to be there. The fire had withered in the early hours of the morning, but it often did. Never had anyone turned to an icicle this way before.

Margaret cupped her hands over her face, gasping for air through the shock. She tugged at his shoulder, begging him to respond. He did not. As Margaret tugged a third time, the hinge in his shoulder cracked, and his arm fell loose, shattering on the ground below.

Still, he did not respond. Margaret stepped back, slicing her foot open on a shard of Gregory's frozen arm.

He did not respond when she slipped. He did not respond when her belly crashed to the floor. He did not respond when Margaret realised this was it.

The baby was coming.

GREGORY'S LEGACY STEPPED ONTO THE ship with a heavy heart. While he'd never met either of his parents, the town often regaled him with tales of the brave engineer who had saved the town's water supply. Uncle Charlie rolled his eyes any time the story was told, muttering how it had been his idea to cull the otters and how Gregory had lapsed into melancholia and been frozen to death by his guilt.

But nobody believed him. In Sioux Falls, you didn't speak ill of the dead. Especially the Cox clan. Poor Margaret – she'd died during childbirth, clutching pieces of her husband's shattered limbs. The gruesome scene had only been discovered some hours later after the screaming baby, surrounded by placental matter and death, had been heard by the neighbours.

Ian slumped up the ramp to the ship, carrying nothing but a small bag of memories, saying a silent goodbye to both sets of parents: the ones who bore him and the ones who raised him.

He'd had a good life here in Sioux Falls, but everyone knew his fate lay elsewhere. Like his father Gregory, Ian grew up with an interest in engineering. He had to go where he was needed, and as such, he boarded the vessel to Botany Bay. Captain James Cook had settled Australia – which meant murdering staggering numbers of the native inhabitants – and was now a celebrated figure across the Western lands. Despite the injustice of the way it had been claimed, the land was ripe with opportunity.

So, with a heavy heart, Ian waved goodbye to his parents as they disappeared into the distance. The last thing he heard his mother say was, "I love you, my boy. I love you, Ian Cox Peck."

FIVE

I FROTHED SOME NEWLY PURCHASED almond milk in my coffee machine as Vegan Shaman performed some kind of ritual in each room of the apartment. I'd watched the first ritual in the living room, right up until the point where he'd undressed and rubbed himself against the furniture. He'd seen my wide eyes filling with fear and explained to me that the ghost of the chicken was marking its territory. One way to slow the spread of its takeover was to mark our own territory in response.

I nodded and let him continue. It had felt like the perfect time for a coffee and maybe a biscuit. As the milk frothed and the coffee seeped out of the machine, I remembered the vegan chocolate biscuits Jethro had stuffed into my bag and reached into the cupboard for the pack.

"Excuse me," I called out. "Um, Mr Vegan, sir?"

Vegan Shaman appeared from the bedroom, pulling on jeans as he walked towards me. "Yes?"

I cleared my throat, trying to ignore the hundreds of questions I had. The most pressing right now was what he'd been doing in my bedroom. "Uh, do you want a biscuit?"

He took one, his thick fingers curling around the chocolate in slow motion as I wondered where his hands had been. I put the biscuits down, resigned to having a coffee without any snacks.

"Th-thank you," I stammered.

Vegan Shaman nodded in response, crumbs of chocolate spreading through his scruffy beard. I waited for him to say something – anything – but he just stood in front of me, half-naked, nodding and chewing.

I sipped my coffee, taking in Vegan Shaman's form. Despite the unkempt beard, he had kind eyes and a nice smile buried in there somewhere. I turned away from him so as not to stare at his chest. The salt-and-pepper hairs were matted with sweat, glistening in the mid-morning sun.

Vegan Shaman noticed my wandering eyes and smiled. Clearly sensing my awkwardness, he leaned over the kitchen counter and said, "Tell me what happened."

I swallowed some coffee. "Mr Vegan, sir –"

He held a hand up to pause me. "Please, no 'sir'. I am just Vegan Shaman."

"Well, I was visiting my uncle's fowl farm, and he wanted me to shoot a chicken. It was his way of manning me up, even though, let's face it, I'm thirty-five, and it's kind of too late."

Vegan Shaman nodded before gesturing for me to continue. He was a good listener, and his eyes sparkled as he stared into my soul.

"So, despite my better judgement..." I took a breath to stave off the tears. "I did it. I shot a poor, defenceless chicken. And it's been haunting me ever since."

"I see," Vegan Shaman whispered. "How did the haunting start?"

I explained the situation in as much detail as possible ... leaving out the parts about urine and faecal matter. Vegan Shaman seemed to be taking mental notes as I spoke.

"...and that takes us to when you arrived, and you know the rest." My coffee had run dry, but I cradled the mug against my chest, soaking up the last remains of its warmth.

We sat silently for a moment, Vegan Shaman staring into the distance. I stared at his lips, a soft red emerging from the salt-and-pepper beard. Something about this man had drawn me in, and I found myself imagining what he might look like if he had cleaned up. Maybe some vegan shampoo through that hair. I could even help, make sure those roots were looked after –

I was shaking off the fantasy, aware of how inappropriate that line of thinking was when I saw a smirk penetrate Vegan Shaman's beard.

He knows. He saw me looking.

If he did, he was far too polite to say anything. Instead, he reached across the kitchen counter for my hand. I was happy to let him hold it, my fingers relaxing at the touch of his soft skin. He caressed the back of my hand with his thumb and smirked again.

"I know this all seems strange." His voice was low, comforting. Warm. "But we can help this spirit. We can end this."

"How?" My heart bounced through my chest, and I wasn't sure if it was the anticipation of ending the haunting or the sensation of Vegan Shaman's thumb tracing circles across my hand.

"We need to bury the bones. Your chicken needs a funeral."

I was about to speak — to say what, I had no idea — when a shadow appeared across the kitchen, plunging us into an unnatural darkness. Out of instinct or fear, I wasn't sure, I looked at Vegan Shaman. He would know what was happening; he would know what to do. His face told a different story as he peered through the darkness with eyebrows raised in confusion.

I squeaked, "What's happening, Vegan Shaman?"

He shook his head, lifting his shoulders in a half-shrug. "I think we should get out of here. Right now."

Slipping his coat back on, he took me by the hand. We ran for the door, tripping over each other in a tangle of limbs and perspiration. Muttering our apologies, we helped each other up, and I tugged at the door handle. But the wooden door felt like stone, unmovable, and as I pulled harder and harder, I saw my name scratched into the wood.

My gravestone.

Vegan Shaman barged me out of the way, banging and kicking at the door with all his might. His physical prowess, while impressive considering my impending death, was useless against the power of the chicken.

We couldn't leave this place.

As I watched the chicken scratch today's date into the wood, I stepped away, looking for somewhere to hide.

In the darkness of the apartment, the stench of chicken faeces filled my nostrils. I gagged at the putrid smell and pulled my shirt over my nose. Vegan Shaman was one step ahead, his nose and mouth covered by an old bandana. He grabbed my shoulder and led me to a corner of the living room, shoving me to the ground beneath the owl clock.

Before I could query his choice, he pointed at the walls around us, filling with scratches and claw marks. They stopped about a foot from the location of the clock – an invisible barrier of some kind. Vegan Shaman had found a slice of safety in the chaos.

He joined me in the corner, huddled close to me as we watched the destruction of the apartment.

"Chickens hate owls," he said. "Amongst other things."

"That's great, but we can't stay here forever," I replied, grimacing at the mess the chicken was making. My couch was torn apart, the fluff spilling to the floor like guts. The walls had been scratched down to the bare timber, the floorboards ripped apart.

Amid the chaos, I wrapped my arms around Vegan Shaman and buried my head in his chest. He cradled me there, caressing my hair. Despite all that went on around us, our piece of safety and the warmth emanating from Vegan Shaman's chest kept my heart from beating itself into extinction.

"You're right," he said after a while. "We can't stay here."

I looked up at him, pleading for him to continue, to have a solution. His eyes were fixed on the kitchen. I could see the cogs turning in his mind, the beginnings of a plan.

"What are you thinking?" I asked, following his gaze.

"Lemons," he said, lips curving to the ceiling.

"Lemons?" I repeated, losing hope. The old shaman had lost it.

He nodded. "Lemons. Tell me you have lemons in that fridge."

"I guess," I shrugged. "But our problems are a bit too big for a lemon drink, don't you think?"

Vegan Shaman smiled again and kissed me quick on the lips. "Lemons!"

He stood up, took the owl clock from its position on the wall, and posed like a knight in battle, the owl his shield.

My knight. I pushed back a smile and refocused.

"Stay behind me," he ordered. "We're going to the kitchen."

The chicken shrieked as we moved from the corner. The shrill cry was deafening, matched only by my own screams. Vegan Shaman held the clock shield before him, pointing it towards the *thud-thud* of ghostly footsteps as the invisible chicken raced towards us. He repelled it each time, but I knew it only made the chicken angrier.

We were halfway to the kitchen when the furniture started to move by itself. A couch cushion was thrust across the room. The table lamp flew towards me and smashed against my ribs. I cried out but did my best to ignore the pain and the blood seeping from my midriff.

I held Vegan Shaman's coat, carefully staying one step behind him as we dodged household items. The couch slid towards us. Vegan Shaman stopped it with a powerful kick. Jethro had been right – he was good – maybe even the best. Whatever he needed lemons for, I was with him all the way. Damn, I'd squeeze him some lemonade if that was what he wanted.

As Vegan Shaman repeatedly repelled the chicken, evading furniture like an Olympic dodgeball player, the chicken's shrill became louder. The walls trembled and shook, pieces of wood swirling in the air as the creature created a windstorm in my living room. The rancid smell of chicken poop hit my face like a punch, and I hoped I wasn't facing a major case of pink eye.

"Almost there!" Vegan Shaman cried over the wind.

Amongst the frenzy, I saw blood and auburn feathers seep from the walls, and I knew if we didn't make it to those lemons soon, we would be as stuffed as a roast chicken.

"Hurry!" I cried, pointing to the blood dripping to the floor and rising from the gaps in the floorboards. Feathers tumbled around us, scratching my face and arms. Vegan Shaman fought the wind current and grabbed the kitchen counter.

The wind increased. I slipped on some blood and loosened my grip on Vegan Shaman's coat. In his effort to breach the kitchen, he didn't notice. As I fell, my fingers slipped from the fabric, and I called his name through the heavy gust.

He didn't hear me.

The wind sped up again, and my body rose into the air. "Vegan Shaman!" I called over and over, but the sound was thrown around the room.

I joined my voice a moment later, tumbling through the air with the contents of my living room. The broken television crashed towards me, its sharp corner slicing my forehead open.

Vegan Shaman made his way into the kitchen, his own body rising into the air. He sacrificed the owl clock to grab the fridge handle and held on with all his might, fighting against the tornado in my living room. He opened the fridge and managed to hold on to the handle as the food flew past him while he searched the fruit drawer. Gripping a single lemon, he tore at the skin with his teeth and smiled when the insides were revealed.

"Suck on this!" he screamed and let go of the fridge.

Joining me in the windy vortex, Vegan Shaman squeezed the lemon. The citrus juice swirled through the air. The chicken shrieked as he squeezed again. The owl clock circled in the wind, and Vegan Shaman grabbed hold of the ceramic shield.

The wind slowed, but the furniture circled in the air, dipping to crash against the walls and the floor. I fought to stay conscious, the wound on my forehead deeper than I thought, and in my haze, I saw Vegan Shaman resume his knight's pose.

Pointing the owl clock towards the centre of the tornado, he bellowed, "You shall not pass!"

Our bodies and the furniture fell to the floor, the wind dissipating to a gentle breeze for a moment before picking up again. I crawled behind Vegan Shaman as he squeezed the last of the lemon into the air, holding it and the owl clock in front of him.

"You shall not pass!" he yelled again, beard flowing in the wind like Falkor – graceful, despite the situation. This time, the wind disappeared, the chicken crying out one last time before re-entering the void it had come from.

Sitting amongst the ruined apartment, Vegan Shaman cursed the chicken a few times before resting back on the floor with heavy breaths.

I held my head. "How did you do that?"

"Chickens hate lemon." He shrugged. "Too citrusy."

"But *one* lemon? Really?"

Vegan Shaman shrugged again and giggled. "They *really* hate lemon."

A *thud-thud-thud* came from the floor beneath us, and Vegan Shaman and I exchanged worried glances. The haunting events hadn't ever been this close together.

"Keep it down up there!" a voice called out. "Fuckin' *Lord of the Rings* bullshit!"

Realising it was only my angry downstairs neighbour, we exhaled and let out relieved laughs.

"Sorry, Mrs Dawson," I called back through my laughter. "I'll turn it down."

We rested amongst the devastation until our breathing regulated. I voiced my concern about the blood still flowing from my forehead. Vegan Shaman took me to the bathroom. He was attentive in his bandaging, and I noticed him steal a few looks as he cared for me.

I cleared my throat. "That kiss before..." I let the sentence hang in the air.

Vegan Shaman smiled again. "I hope that was okay."

I nodded with as much passion as I could muster with a wounded and throbbing head. "I just didn't know if it was adrenaline or something else."

"A bit of both, I think. You've captivated me."

I didn't know what to say, so I let his words filter through the air. The stench of chicken poop remained, and I knew it was a sign that the fowl beast would be back. That it hadn't ever left. My brain tingled at the thought that the chicken was watching and listening to us.

As nice as it was to have a reprieve from the haunting, and as much as I wanted to pursue a romance with Vegan

Shaman, I couldn't afford to be sidetracked – not just yet. I bookmarked my interest in him for later and refocused on the matter at hand.

As the last of the bandage was wrapped around my head, I asked him, "You mentioned something about a burial?"

Vegan Shaman rested against the bathroom wall. "We have to make things right. Call your uncle. We need to go back to where this all started. We need to go back to the farm."

PART III

THE EMU WAR OF 1932 in Western Australia had left dark stains on flightless birds across the country, though the horrors of the military-run genocide had not died with the laying down of the guns. The humans moved on to killing each other again, forgetting about the emus almost altogether, other than to gaze upon them in cages at zoos. The emus, however, did not move on. The war may have been over, both sides returning to their respective enemy lines, but casualties continued to be found, splayed across the dirt and the bloodstained grass as warnings to the emus who still dared to breathe.

In 1950, descendants of the war's survivors were culled by farmers who claimed the presence of the birds threatened their crops and, by proxy, their existence. Emus had once again become synonymous with evil in the desert state of Western Australia. The audacity and arrogance of the humans left lasting stains in ancestral emu blood, stories conveyed through rock scrawls and whispered over howling winds on rainy nights.

No, the emus had not moved on. The war was not over. The stories became infrequent as time passed, but the hatred pulsing through the emus' blood remained. Hatred for humankind everywhere. The little ones were the worst, throwing stones and sharp sticks at the infant emus who cowered behind their defenceless mothers. The little ones would be the first to go, but not yet.

Time was a powerful thing. It passed of its own accord, watched society change and crumble as industry continued to sweep the land. Roads were built on the very farmland the emu ancestors had died on. The farmland once worth killing over. Gravesites were forgotten under layers of concrete and tar and human selfishness.

Word of the war had of course crossed deserts and rivers, a folktale among emus everywhere. The power of time had seen the tale spread like a virus until every emu, caged or free, had a penetrating hatred for the human monsters. One emu, born into captivity on the eve of the humans' New Year celebration, felt the rage of his ancestors bubbling in his veins.

The emu lived with his brothers and sisters, who seemed content with their captivity, scratching their feathers on a barbed wire fence and eating what the human warden provided. Licking their beaks with greed in their bellies. The emu would watch from afar – the proverbial black sheep, as humans would say – and plan.

Plan the escape.

The emu's ancestors would not have been content with grass and insects dealt out at some human's discretion. They would not have lazed around while the small humans burped in their faces and made horrible high-pitched squeals, throwing seeds, and ordering them to eat. Today's emus had been bred to depend on the creatures that craved their demise.

The emu did not like humans.

The emu would leave this place.

Even if he had to kill.

ISABELLA AWOKE WITH A LUMP in her neck and a pain in her shoulders. The pain she had come to trust. For she knew that if she awoke with these two symptoms, her dream was not a conjuring of her unconscious mind. Her dream was a warning.

Lifting the bedcovers and stretching her arms above her head, Isabella contemplated the dream. Vivid imagery replayed on her eyelids, chills running over her arms as the emotions of the creature in her dream solidified in her own soul.

No, she thought. *Not a creature.* "An emu."

Isabella rushed to her phone book and searched. She knew of an emu farm in northern Queensland, but experience with these matters told her not to jump the gun. *Do the research and fact-check. Make sure all the signs point to yes.* In her dream, the location looked remote. It didn't seem to be a city-based zoo or an enclosure. It was a farm. Open spaces, green fields with a stream and every comfort the emus might want. They should be happy there.

But the feeling rushed to her gut again. A dark, intense

hatred. Swallowing the lump in her throat, Isabella knew that the emu farm was the right place. She had to get there fast before it was too late.

Isabella lived quite a distance from the emu farm. It was going to be a long drive – maybe all day. The sun was still lugging itself to the horizon, so she felt there was enough time. The dream had taken place at night. She had a good twelve hours before the emu would attack. With that knowledge, she jumped into her beat-up old Toyota Corolla and headed for the emu farm.

JEREMY WIPED HIS EYES AND took a deep breath. The hours he'd been putting in were becoming a joke. Illegal, even. His boss, Mr Schreiner, the German twat, refused to pay overtime and had threatened Jeremy's job when he'd queried doing a fifty-hour week.

"You want money, yes?" Schreiner had said in his usual blunt tone.

"Yes, sir, I –"

"You want money, you do work."

The shrug had bothered Jeremy, but Schreiner turning his back was a big "F you" that the young man could not understand. He'd waited by Schreiner's back for a moment, building the courage to argue, but instead had followed his pride out of the man's office.

That had been several days before when logic had not yet dissolved from Jeremy's moral toolkit. Today was a different story, though, and the hours of lost sleep had coalesced under his eyeballs as black circles. His face was gaunt and yellowed from a lack of vitamins and protein.

He'd had the peculiar feeling that one of the emus was watching him. Learning his rhythms and habits. Now, as he headed for the sanctuary to refill the hay, the eyes were on him again. Those red, expressionless emu eyes. Jeremy looked at the creature and smiled, sure that it understood his peaceful gesture.

It tilted its head and stepped closer, its three-toed foot scratching at the dusty earth. As sure as he was that the creature understood his smile, he was also sure it was sizing him up. Gauging the strength of his character. The strength of his muscles.

The strength of his pulse.

Jeremy's chores were performed on autopilot, the stench of emu crap his only real measure of reality. The emu glared at him from across the sanctuary. Unblinking. Unmoving.

The day dwindled away, as did Jeremy's energy levels and care factor. His shift was almost over, though the threat of more overtime lingered in his nostrils next to the emu crap. His thoughts of avoiding Schreiner distracted him as he exited the sanctuary for the final time that day, leaving the gate unlocked.

Sluggish, Jeremy wandered to his car, practicing his "I can't tonight" for Schreiner. He didn't notice the emu's beak working at the gate. He didn't notice the emu kicking the metal door open. He didn't hear its clawed feet clop along the concrete towards him.

A car pulled into the emu farm's car park, headlights glowing in the dying daylight. Jeremy watched the car, ignoring the scraping sound behind him. A woman, maybe in her thirties, waved at him, pointed and screamed. He couldn't hear her words through the car window and decided it was best to ignore her, too.

The car skidded towards him, showing no signs of stopping. Jeremy ducked for cover, crying out, "Crazy bitch!" as he dove out of its path.

He landed on his shoulder, letting out an involuntary "Oof" as the emu towered over him. For the first time, Jeremy felt validated that his feelings were right. The emu had been watching him. It *knew* him.

He smiled at it, extending a hand to the animal in friendship. Before he could speak, the emu's beak stabbed at his hand, severing it from his wrist. The emu spat the meat to the pavement, blood dripping from its greedy mouth, and stepped towards the young man.

Jeremy's scream, it would be said later, was heard several kilometres away. It would also be said that the emu had shredded the man's vocal cords in the seconds that followed, sending a horrible quiet through the humid Queensland night air, before it fled into the nearby bushes.

THE CAR SCREECHED TO A halt as the emu rushed into the bushes, the young man's vocal cords flailing from its mouth. Isabella barged the car door with her shoulder – the only way it opened these days – and rushed to the man's side. Falling to her knees, she pressed against the gaping wound in his neck, trying to seal the gap where skin used to be. Her fingers sank into the shredded cartilage. The young man's eyes were wide with fear, staring at her, pleading for help they both knew would be too late.

Isabella watched the life fade from his eyes, and when he stopped choking on his own blood, she knew his time was over. The emu was nowhere to be seen, but Isabella felt it was still close. Was it lingering beyond the trees, watching her? Waiting?

"The hell happened here?"

A voice broke the silence, and Isabella searched the empty parking lot. A man had appeared in the shadows by the farm's main entrance, carrying a spear. In the dim light, it looked homemade.

"I heard screaming and –"

Isabella turned back to the dead young man and pressed his eyelids down as heavy footsteps rushed to her back.

"Jeremy?" The man prodded at the body with the pointy end of his spear. "Get up."

"I'm sorry," Isabella said, guiding the spear away from Jeremy, "but your friend is dead."

"What –?" He choked, left his words unfinished. Bent down to get a closer look at the body.

"He was attacked. By an emu." Isabella motioned towards the bushes. "It escaped through there."

The man straightened, wiped his eyes and marched to the trees, the grip on his spear so tight that his fingers had lost all colour. Isabella rushed after him, wiping her hands on the back of her clothes.

"What are you going to do?" she asked as she caught up to him.

"The emu must die."

Trudging through the dark woods in silence, the duo was more alert to the sounds of nature than had ever been. Crickets chirping, birds humming, owls waking with soft hoots. Twigs cracking underfoot –

Looking down, Isabella saw no twigs beneath their feet.

"Did you hear that?" she whispered.

The man nodded, peered through the trees. "There."

"Don't hurt it." Isabella tugged on his arm.

He shook her off and glared at her. "You have nothing to do with this. Leave now."

Isabella let the man walk ahead, unsure what to do. Her dream had ended well before this point. There was no guidance in the stars tonight, but her gut told her the emu had to live. She followed the man's footsteps, intent on catching the emu, or letting it escape again. She hadn't decided.

The man crept towards the emu. Its back was to him, its long neck bent towards the grass. The poor thing was hungry. It just wanted to be left alone to eat. Isabella tried not to remind herself of the human flesh it had eaten not so long ago. She told herself that it was an animal, that it didn't have a sense of justice – not in the way humans did. Morality was a human concept, after all. It couldn't be held responsible for its actions.

Sucking a worm into its bloodstained beak, the emu raised its neck, putting a target square on its proverbial back. The man readied the spear and before Isabella could intervene – push him, distract him, yell, anything – the spear sailed through the air.

Time moved at a snail's pace for Isabella as she watched the spear plunge into the emu's feathered body.

Watched its beak open, its eyes widen in surprise and pain. Watched it fall to the green earth.

"What have you done?" Isabella screamed, running to the fallen animal.

The emu screeched an unbearable noise through the trees as Isabella sat beside it, caressing its brow and neck. Shushing it into an everlasting sleep. The man appeared behind her and tugged at the spear. The emu screeched again as the weapon was plucked from its body. Blood gushed from the site, and the man knelt down with a smile.

"The emu will die." He repeated it like a mantra as if he'd gotten justice for Jeremy.

Again, Isabella watched. She watched the man touch the wound. Watched him taste the blood. Watched the emu's pupils dilate. Watched its chest sink and fail to rise.

Watched the light emerge from its body.

At that moment, Isabella's moral compass faltered. She hated that man so full of vengeance in his heart, a hunter eager to taste his prey. She wanted him to suffer the way he had made the emu suffer. She wanted justice.

The light was brief, and Isabella knew from the man's unchanged expression that he had not seen it. Not everyone could see that sort of thing, just as not everyone had premonitions. But she had seen it –

the light. Most lights of this nature were bright white, some a little dimmer if the death had been early. On rare occasions, the light was darker. The colour of misery. The colour of an unhappy soul. This was such an occasion.

Despite her desire for justice, Isabella tried to warn the man. She tried to tell him that the emu's soul was lingering for revenge. Her words fell on ears that did not want to listen. Her intentions were met with a sneer and a shove as he headed back to the farm.

"You need to listen," she begged. But his footsteps were already far away.

Isabella wrapped her arms around the dead emu's neck, apologising for its violent end. Guiding the creature's light towards the sky, instead of towards the man.

It was no good.

His screams gave Isabella the incentive to leave the emu behind. She raced through the bushes, tripping over rocks and fallen branches in the dark, stopping only when she came across the man's severed limbs jutting out of the earth. Entrails decorated the leaves around her, a pool of red seeping into the dirt and grass underfoot.

She saw the emu's apparition burping on the man's stomach and slapped her hands to her mouth. It was enough to be heard by the angry spirit, which turned to face her. The eyes, red and empty, watched her. It tilted its head to her, seemed to be considering her fate.

Music swept through the woods, faint but persistent. The words of "Happy Birthday" drifted towards them, and as the rhythm fell on the words "to you", the emu vanished.

Isabella stood at the crime scene for a few moments, absorbing the violence and the rage of the creature. This was no ordinary spirit. This one couldn't be saved.

The song continued, pulling Isabella from her thoughts. A group of campers must be nearby, celebrating, and her gut insisted that the emu would be heading there now. Tearing through the bushes towards the singing, Isabella hoped beyond hope that she could get there in time.

She must be getting close. She could hear distinct voices now. Her panicked ears couldn't tell how many, but there were quite a few. If she didn't hurry, the emu would kill them all.

THE CAMPSITE CONSISTED OF SEVERAL log cabins splayed around in a semicircle facing the lake. Felled trees had been arranged as seating around a fire pit not far from the shore. Water lapped at the pebbled beach as the three families cosied up around the warm fire.

Aunt Jill and Uncle Rob had been married forever and bickered the way people did when they'd spent too much time together. Uncle Eric and Aunt Alice weren't married yet, but a huge ring on her finger told the world of their intentions. Alice was always harping about the wedding and asking if so-and-so had returned the RSVP slip. Another two, Sarah and Tim, cuddled together, staring in silence at the events unfolding around them.

A young boy adopted the same approach and watched the group: Jill and Rob wrapping blankets around themselves, Eric swearing as he opened a beer, and the fizz covered his shoes. Alice always laughed at him, but the boy didn't see what was so funny. He didn't care if he was being honest. There were more important things going on tonight.

He sat on his hands, something his mother – Sarah – always reminded him to do whenever he was excited. And, well, it was his birthday, so the kid was about as enthusiastic as he'd ever been. He was turning the big six, and then he wouldn't be the youngest in his class anymore. He couldn't wait to see Jade in the schoolyard on Monday and poke fun at her for being born later than him.

A few times he thought he'd heard noises from the woods beyond, but he was a big kid now, so he wasn't allowed to be scared by weird noises. Nobody else had seemed to notice, so he went about his business, keeping a distant eye on the tree line.

His mother winked at him as they sat around the fire, his uncles and aunts all yammering on about something or another. Of course, they weren't really his aunts and uncles. It was just something his mum said. His father would just roll his eyes and go along with it in between long sucks on a cigarette.

The boy didn't mind being the only kid there. It made him feel superior to the other kids – of everyone in the whole world, *he* got to sit in the fire circle with the adults. All the other babies had to go to bed when the sun went down.

Smirking at the thought, the boy didn't notice his mother walking towards him from the cabin. He didn't notice her carrying something or the sparkles flickering in the night. His father pointed and the boy rejoiced when he recognised the item his mother carried.

Birthday cake. The best kind of cake.

The group gathered round and filled the night with soft serenades and birthday wishes. The boy beamed from ear to ear at the attention and affection, his father's arm loose around his shoulders and Aunt Jill pinching his cheeks every few seconds. It kind of hurt, but he liked it anyway.

Sucking in a deep breath, the boy was readying himself to blow out the sparklers when he saw the darkness emerge from the woods. A shadow that moved on its own. He pointed to the shadow converging on the group in silence. His mother and father exchanged glances – the boy couldn't read what their faces said – and Aunt Jill and Uncle Rob dove to the ground.

The shadow loomed above them, and even though his mother had covered his eyes, the boy watched through the gaps in her fingers. The shadow changed shape into some kind of animal. He'd seen pictures of these at school. It was an emu.

Emus were okay. They were harmless, his teacher had said.

But as the dark shadow changed into a beast with red eyes, it didn't look harmless.

His mother grabbed him by the waist, hauled him over her shoulder and ran for the cabin. He heard her panting and felt her trembling as she struggled with the door handle. His father was nowhere to be seen, and the boy searched the campsite for the rest of his family.

The creature stepped into the fire without reacting. The orange glow spread through its body as though the flames offered it strength. The cabin door swung open, and the boy was thrown across the room onto the bed.

"Hide!" his mother ordered in a harsh whisper. Her voice had an urgency he'd never heard before.

The boy scrambled under the bed, peering towards the door. His mother slammed it shut, and the boy heard her footsteps disappear towards the campfire. Just like that, she was gone.

He heard voices outside. Aunt Jill called for help. Uncle Eric screamed. He was saying something, but his voice sounded so pained and panicked that the words came out as ramblings. The boy heard a gunshot. Another one.

Who had a gun? he thought and crawled further under the bed.

The cries for help were too much to bear. The boy listened for his mother and father, tried to hear their voices amongst the chaos outside. Between the screeching of the creature and the screams of his family, the boy could not tell the difference. He couldn't recognise anybody's voice.

A new voice entered his hearing. A woman. She sounded kind but scared. Her words also made no sense, but in a different way to Uncle Eric's. Her words weren't garbled – they were in another language. Something about them seemed powerful. Her voice gained strength with each word.

The screams dissipated until only the woman's voice remained.

The boy crawled from under the bed and tiptoed to the cabin door. He didn't want to disobey his mother by coming out, but he wanted to know that everyone was okay. They'd stopped their screaming, after all. Maybe the creature had gotten bored and left.

He opened the door, only a little, to peer through the crack. He didn't see his mother, father, or family. The ground looked wet, but there hadn't been any rain. The woman he'd heard talking was standing in a puddle, drenched, shouting words towards the creature. The creature looked in pain and tried to move towards the woman but fell to the ground. The sound it made was indescribable and haunting.

Opening the door wider and stepping into the night air, the boy saw the ground was not wet with water. The earth had turned red, and the puddle was a deep crimson, too. He stepped onto the ground, recoiling at the squishing red mud between his toes, and scanned the campsite for his parents.

As she stood above the creature, the woman yelled more words in that unfamiliar language. She held something in her hands, like a crucifix, but different. As she pushed the object into the creature's face, it made that horrible screech once more and vanished – just like that. One second, it was there; the next, it was gone.

He watched her fall to her knees and sob. Her shoulders bounced up, and down the way, the boy's mother did when she fought with his father. He walked towards her and laid a hand on her shoulder.

"Have you seen my mummy and daddy?" he asked. He knew she was upset. He should have asked if she was okay, but he was worried about his parents.

The woman looked at him and told him to close his eyes. She embraced the boy in her wet arms and clothes, begging him not to look. He didn't know what he was supposed to be avoiding. What it was that she didn't want him to see. As the woman sobbed harder, the boy stared into the red earth, finally understanding that it was not water making the mud under his feet.

"That thing killed them, didn't it?" the boy whispered, holding back tears.

"I'm sorry, my boy," was all the woman could stutter.

He closed his eyes and hugged her back.

They embraced until the tears dried up and the mud

started to harden under the sun of a new day. The woman took the boy by the hand and led him through the woods. They walked and walked until the boy's bare feet blistered and a car park came into view through the trees.

Police cars lined the nearby street, yellow tape strung about the place. The woman told the boy to sneak into a beaten-up Toyota Corolla, assuring him she would meet him soon. Nobody noticed him walking through the crime scene barefoot and wearing bloodstained pyjamas.

He climbed into the car and waited. He saw the woman speaking to a policeman, gesturing down to her clothes. The boy noticed then that her clothes were red, but he could tell they shouldn't have been. His six-year-old brain didn't have the vocabulary to name the feelings he was experiencing, but as he watched the woman wring blood from her sleeve and the policeman comfort her with a gentle hand on the shoulder, he began to process what had happened.

Mummy. Daddy. Dead.

The woman returned to the car looking haggard and fragile and climbed into the driver's seat. She gripped the steering wheel, white knuckles almost bursting from her skin. Her breathing was strange, sometimes fast, sometimes slow – too slow. The boy let her breathe for a while until he couldn't stand the silence anymore.

"What do I do now?" He wiped his eyes, cheeks flushed from a new wave of tears.

"Come with me," the woman said, brushing dirty hair from her face. "My name is Isabella, but you can call me Mama Shaman."

SIX

On the drive up to the farm, I had the luxury of the passenger seat. I'd called Uncle John to let him know I was on my way back. The cheer in his tone was louder than his voice as he screamed over the tractor engine, and I felt a pang of regret that I'd run off the way I did. We talked for a few minutes over the roar of the engine before saying our goodbyes.

"Wait," I said in a hurry, "before you go – what did you do with the chicken I... murdered?"

Uncle John laughed. "Murder? That's a bit rough, mate. It's just a chicken."

I was glad not to be on loudspeaker, worried what Vegan Shaman would think of my only living relative. "What did you do with it?"

"Chucked it in the bin." I could hear the lack of care in his voice. He didn't understand at all. Maybe he couldn't afford to since mass murder was his livelihood.

"Can you get it out, please?"

Silence.

"My friend and I need to bury it."

I heard Uncle John stifle another laugh, but he agreed to do as I asked.

I ended the call, leaned back in the passenger seat, and closed my eyes. Despite it being only day two of the haunting, I felt as though I hadn't slept for years. The sun was starting to sink beneath the purple-and-orange horizon, the earth's way of saying a slow goodnight.

Vegan Shaman told me without explanation that he didn't like the radio, so we travelled silently for a few kilometres until it became deafening. This man had entered my life only hours earlier and had saved my life twice.

"How old are you?" I asked.

"Forty-one," he replied. When I raised my eyebrows in disbelief, he continued, "In my line of work, you tend to age a little faster than the average."

"How long have you been shamaning?" I tripped on the word. "Shaman-nan-ing?"

Vegan Shaman giggled at that and reached into his shirt to expose a necklace. It held a locket he told me to open as he passed it to me. Clicking the pendant open, I saw an old photo: a man, a woman, and a small child embracing around a campfire. The man wore parachute pants and a brightly coloured tie-dyed shirt, while the woman sported a flowery dress, a guitar resting against her leg. They held the child on their laps, all smiling. I gathered the child was Vegan Shaman.

"My parents used to take me to this camping spot for my birthday every year. That photo was taken on my sixth birthday. Back then, there was an emu farm, but it was fully secure, and there weren't any issues we knew about."

He stared at the road before him as he spoke, as though the memories played out in the beams of light against the tarmac. I sat in silence, waiting for him to continue.

"This one year, one of the emus got out, so it had to be put down. And – well, you think the ghost of your chicken is mad...."

"What happened?"

Vegan Shaman took a deep breath, wiped his eyes, and said, "The emu's ghost went on a rampage. Killed eight people that night. I barely got away."

I scanned my memory of the Reddit threads I'd devoured earlier. Pieces of his story rang around my grey matter until I found the source material. Queensland, Australia. 1981. A communal camping village had been attacked by the angry spirit of an emu that had been speared through the heart after escaping the local emu farm. As Vegan Shaman had said, eight people had been ripped apart, their limbs chewed up and spat out like rotten meat. According to Reddit, two survivors were there that night: the shaman who had exorcised the spirit and a small child.

"The shaman who saved me took me in after that and taught me her ways. I've been a shaman ever since that night."

I let the tragic story settle into my bones for a few minutes, unable to fathom the reality of family members being torn apart by a ghost – let alone the ghost of an emu. It was clear why Vegan Shaman was so passionate about his career – he didn't want anyone else to go through what he had.

"My parents are gone, too," I said in a feeble attempt at solidarity.

"You should rest." Vegan Shaman's voice was soft against the hum of tires on the tarmac. I looked at him. My sunken eyes must have betrayed me, for he rested a gentle hand on my thigh and said, "Get some sleep. I won't let anything happen to you."

Maybe the permission to rest did it, or Vegan Shaman's reassuring hand on my leg, but as I leaned my head against the window, sleep came quickly.

SEVEN

UNCLE JOHN WAVED AT US from the end of the driveway, his canine companion, Ruby, a few steps behind him, barking through her excitement. An Old English Sheepdog, she loved to keep the chickens and other assorted creatures in line with a snarl or a nip. Ruby had never been too excited to see me, so now I was a taken aback by her enthusiasm.

I was even more taken aback that she was here. Ruby had died several years earlier in a horrible tractor incident.

"Cute dog," Vegan Shaman said.

"Y-Yeah," I stammered. "Except she's dead."

Vegan Shaman considered my words for a moment as he scanned the area. He sensed something, I could tell. I asked after the thoughts rolling through his brain.

"If your uncle's dog has passed over and we can see her now…" His words were slow, careful. "The chicken may be drawing its power from other spirits in the area. We must be approaching the nexus of its rage."

I gulped.

"What happened back at your apartment was only a taste of its true power."

Gulping again, I searched the car for lemons. I was sure Vegan Shaman had packed some.

"I'm afraid we're beyond lemons now," he whispered. "I have one in my pocket, just in case."

I sensed his fear as we continued up the long driveway towards the farm. Uncle John waved again, coming down to greet us. Poor Uncle John. He had no idea. We clambered out of the car, and his smile dropped when he noticed my bandaged head and the slashes on my arms and face.

He gripped my shoulders and examined my wounds. "What happened to you?" His concern was deep and real. I felt the love pouring from him and it took all I had not to crumble into a mess of tears right then and there.

"The chicken," Vegan Shaman interrupted. "The murdered chicken did this to your nephew."

Uncle John sized the shaman up, scepticism oozing from his eyes. He ignored Vegan Shaman and turned back to me for an answer.

I shrugged. "What he said."

"I assure you, I am no crackpot." Vegan Shaman took off his hat and bowed to my uncle. "Despite some cracks in my face here and there."

I shook my head, an indication for him to please just *try* to be more normal. First impressions are critical. Before my uncle could respond to Vegan Shaman in any way, I ushered them both towards the house, ignoring Ruby's playful nuzzling at the back of my knee.

Exhaustion still pulsed through my veins, and I was glad to make it to the living room, where the sofa beckoned me. I collapsed into the soft fabric and rested my eyes again, listening to the conversation between Uncle John and Vegan Shaman unfold.

"Rubbish." Uncle John dismissed the shaman's insistence about the haunting.

"Have you noticed anything strange since the death of the chicken?" Vegan Shaman pressed.

"Yes," Uncle John replied. "A crazy shaman appeared at my front door after brainwashing my nephew!"

I heard the deep breaths from both men and saw where this was headed – two blokes in a punch-up and me an easy target for this chicken's wrath. My head throbbed with disappointment and the pressure of all the coagulating blood, so I let the argument continue and walked out of the room, heading for the bathroom. I needed to take a shower, clean up some of this dried blood, and freshen up my bandages.

Ruby barked amongst the chaos in the living room, and I heard Vegan Shaman snap at the dog as I shut the bathroom door. They would sort it out eventually, I was sure. But for now, I needed some peace and quiet and some piping-hot water cascading across my pale, battered skin.

I unwrapped the bandage from my head. As the bloodstained gauze fell to the floor, my head ached. My vision went fuzzy. I felt like an old television from the 1980s, trying to get a picture out of snow. Maybe slapping the side of my head would yield a better result, but I wasn't brave enough to try. Instead, I undressed, reached past the shower curtain and turned the tap.

Uncle John had invested in a gas system a few years prior, so the heat was instantaneous. The bathroom filled with steam, warm and moist against my skin. Hot water spilled from the showerhead, the pressure like needles. Just what I needed.

I rubbed dried blood from the half-sealed gash on my forehead and watched the red liquid circle the drain. I had hoped the steam and hot water might rejuvenate me, but as the water spiralled in my fuzzy vision, the tension in my head began to build again.

Ignore it.

Reaching for the shampoo, I squinted at the label to see if it was vegan. No such luck. I risked it anyway, conscious that the blood, sweat, and grime were not just through my hair. I squeezed a generous amount of shampoo into my palm. I almost felt the lifeforms growing in my armpits, wriggling in discomfort as I rubbed shampoo through the wiry hair.

I was starting to feel better, less tense, as the dirt and grime were swept down the drain, and the scent of pomegranate overtook the stench of days-old sweat. Massaging the shampoo into my scalp, I felt something unfamiliar amongst the hair.

Pulling at it with my thumb and forefinger, I brought an auburn feather to my face.

Must have been from the tornado.

I dropped it and continued to massage my scalp. Relished the self-pampering with a soft whistle of "Singin' in the Rain". Just as the whistle mutated into song, I felt something else shift in my hair. My head ached. Something was scratching inside my brain. It pushed out and crept down my neck to brushed against my shoulders.

I spun around, knowing I was alone but not quite believing it.

"Hello?"

Classic mistake. The chicken doesn't speak.

Nothing was there, but I knew by now that I hadn't imagined it. The chicken was coming for me. My head burned again, and I screamed in pain as the scratching continued. It was the chicken. It was inside me. Its wings had emerged from the back of my head. Devil wings.

My knees buckled as the chicken forced its way out of my skull, its beak clawing at flesh and bone. I cried for help, but over the running water and their continued arguing, neither my uncle nor my shaman heard my pleas.

The pain was intolerable now, my vision all but gone as the pressure continued to fill my head It felt like the chicken was hatching from my skull, cracking me apart little by little. Once more, one of its wings brushed against my shoulder, and I snatched at it. Feathers in my grip, I yanked.

The chicken tumbled to the wet floor with an angry cry, its auburn feathers deepening to black under the steady flow of hot water. I pressed myself into the corner of the shower, all too aware that I had several inches on display. A worm for the chicken.

Please, please, please. I couldn't speak the words, just shouted them in my mind. *Not my worm!*

I cradled myself in my hands, a feeble attempt to save the children once again, and called for Vegan Shaman. Called for Uncle John. He'd have to believe us now. The chicken *brrrk*ed and clucked, pecking towards me with hunger and hatred in its eyes.

Knowing I could only count on myself this time, I kicked at the chicken, landing a toe in its beak. I kicked again, kept kicking until it was out of shower, disappearing through the steam.

Turning the shower off, I waited in the silence for a noise. A scratch, a cluck, anything that would tell me the chicken's location. Peering through the steam, I saw a shadow, like a hand coming towards me. Its wing, outstretched like a series of daggers. Five blades, coming for my soul.

I stopped breathing.

Peered through the shower curtain.

The shadow landed on the plastic in front of me, growing as the chicken approached. Was this my fate? Was I Janet Leigh in the chicken edition of *Psycho*? No. I knew I could fight back. I'd had it in me moments ago to kick the chicken, and I had it in me now.

The shower curtain was my only defence. As the chicken scratched its way towards me, I tore the curtain from its rod and rushed forward.

The dagger-wings fought at the plastic, tearing holes and puncturing my arms, but I tightened the curtain around its body. I heard it cluck and cry as it struggled, strengthening my resolve as I crushed it into a ball.

I was no Janet Leigh. Jamie Lee could put down a monster.

I lifted the balled-up chicken and thrust it against the bathroom mirror. Shards of glass cut my feet and ankles. I ignored the pain, invigorated now that I had finally taken the upper hand. I smashed the chicken against the tiled walls and the floor against the vanity. Threw it around the bathroom like a rubber ball until it made no sound.

A mess of panting and sweat, I couldn't help but feel my shower had been a waste of time. I hadn't even rinsed the shampoo. The pomegranate scent did give me some comfort.

I kicked the chicken once more for good measure.

Blotches of deep red seeped onto my hands through the rips and tears in the shower curtain. I could smell the dense iron in the chicken's blood and was overcome by that same sense of guilt I'd had when I first killed him.

As I unwrapped the curtain to reveal a wreck of broken bones, I saw the chicken's eye – staring wide at me.

I dared it to do something. But it lay there, brittle and broken and defeated. I rested back on the bathroom tiles, careful to avoid splintering my butt cheeks with shards of glass.

A deep pride washed over me as I sat amongst the mess. While the chicken may have started as an innocent creature, it was innocent no more. Rage did funny things to people, and to chickens, I supposed – emus, too, as the Vegan Shaman told it. There could be something to say about being a vegan. I'd lived the experience that told me animals of all different types could feel emotion and cared enough about their deaths to haunt people.

And kill, I reminded myself.

A *tap-tap* on the bathroom door drew me from my thoughts. Uncle John and Vegan Shaman exchanged glances in the doorway as they frowned upon my naked form and the mess I'd made.

"What the –" Uncle John began.

"I did it." I looked to Vegan Shaman and pointed at the chicken. "I destroyed it."

Vegan Shaman stepped into the bathroom, both of us ignoring my uncle's continued "Hello?"s and "Can somebody answer me?"s. As Vegan Shaman crept closer to the chicken, brow furrowed, he mumbled something under his breath. It sounded like a prayer.

I was so focused on him that I almost failed to notice the trail of blood leaking towards me over the shattered glass. A thick stream of dark liquid came towards me, purposeful. Just as Vegan Shaman cried out to warn me, the blood reached my hand.

"Get it off me!" I screamed, pointing at the liquid now running up my arm.

Vegan Shaman stepped back, his expression betraying that he had no idea what was happening. Uncle John stood in disbelief in the doorway, arms crossed, muttering "Just being a little bit of blood, for God's sake," and "This is what I meant about manning up."

The blood raced up my arm, across my shoulder and chin, moving towards my mouth. I closed my lips and squeezed as tight as I could, but the blood forced its way through minuscule gaps. I tasted it as it soaked across my tongue, filling my mouth for a moment before spilling down my throat. I grabbed at my mouth and neck, choking, my eyes watering. I could feel the blood filling my lungs, taking hold of every organ. Taking hold of what made me *me*.

Vegan Shaman clasped his hands over his mouth as I began to shake and convulse. My uncle raced towards me, clearly no longer caring whether this was the work of the chicken or some mental illness. He held me in his arms as I convulsed, whispering soothing reassurances as I began to lose consciousness.

Uncle John and Vegan Shaman crowded around my still body, leaning into my chest to sense a heartbeat.

"He's alive," Vegan Shaman said.

Uncle John asked, "What happened?"

Before either man could speak again, my eyes opened.

I could see them kneeling around me, but as I tried to speak, to tell them I was okay, my body wouldn't obey. It was as though I were a passenger in my body, viewing my life on a projector with no way of interacting.

I felt my body stand, my head turn from side to side, and my mouth open.

Brrrrrrrkk.

BATHROOM TILES EXPLODED THROUGH THE air as Harry shrieked. Vegan Shaman ducked low to the ground, cowering beneath the chicken's rage, his hands over his head and face. Harry's uncle crawled towards the door, a trail of blood behind him as shards of glass and tiles dug into the frail skin of his elbows.

Harry's voice twisted into something unrecognizable as the chicken bellowed from his mouth. As Vegan Shaman looked up through the gaps in his fingers, he saw glass and tiles fly across the room – until the chicken fell silent. The shards hung in the air, held in place by an invisible force.

"Vegan Shaman!" John called with a wave. "Get out of there!"

Vegan Shaman shook his head in defiance, unwilling to leave Harry's body at the mercy of the chicken. He knew all too well what would happen if the chicken possessed the human body for too long. They were fighting for Harry's soul now, and the chicken grew stronger with each second it was inside the young man.

Vegan Shaman called out, "Get the bones!"

John wasted no time. Vegan Shaman watched as he cradled his bleeding elbows, got to his feet and bolted through the house towards the bin outside. He hoped the man would do as he'd promised and get the chicken corpse.

Harry watched as his uncle raced outside but did not move. Vegan Shaman suspected the chicken was still growing accustomed to the human body. Couldn't walk yet. This was his chance – maybe the only chance he'd get.

He rose, squeezed his hands into fists, and punched poor Harry in the face.

The body stumbled, and Vegan Shaman punched again before the chicken could do anything at all. And again. He punched Harry's face until his knuckles were raw, and the body stopped moving.

Vegan Shaman looked down upon the frail body, sorrowful. Poor Harry's handsome face would have a lot of bruises when this was over.

EIGHT

HARRY WAS STRUNG ACROSS THE bed like a defiled version of Jesus, both arms outstretched and shackled to the bedposts. There hadn't been time to put clothes on him, but Vegan Shaman had placed a towel to protect his modesty. Harry's head hung limp. He was still unconscious from the beating a few minutes earlier. Vegan Shaman wiped sweat from his forehead as he tied the last knots around Harry's ankles. He was sure the chicken would stir soon, and he knew it absorbed Harry's soul with each passing second.

They didn't have long to save him.

Ruby jumped onto the bed, barking ceaselessly at the possessed young man. The noise shattered Vegan Shaman's eardrums. He yelled at the canine spirit, though he felt guilty, knowing the animal was on their side. Ruby obeyed, retreating to a corner of the bedroom with an angry growl.

Looking upon Harry's form, the Vegan Shaman scratched his head. The usual cases he took were much simpler than this – even the young girl possessed by her hamster. All that had taken was a few pellets and a spin on a Ferris wheel. This one, though, was like nothing he'd faced before.

He reached into the breast pocket of his jacket and pulled out a worn black book. It contained notes on demonic presence and possession, instructions for rituals, recipes of all spiritual kinds, Latin phrases – everything he needed, complete with almost professional imagery. Some pages were torn, some were missing completely, and others had been filled out by his shaman mother in a version of English he couldn't read.

"I wish you were here now," he whispered at the thought of her.

"Who?" Harry's uncle stood in the doorway, holding the chicken bones.

Vegan Shaman sighed and waved the thought away. He considered the options and thought about what they knew so far. Even with all the chicken had done, its motivations were unclear. There was no pattern to the haunting events other than their increasing intensity. Human poltergeists were easy. They possessed people for specific reasons, which would become clear with a short conversation – if you could follow that conversation through all the cursing and insults. But this was different: chickens couldn't speak.

He flipped through the pages of his book, searching for an answer that might help them. Harry started to stir, drooling as he lifted his head to meet Vegan Shaman's gaze. The two remained silent, staring at one another, daring the other to make the first move. Whatever that move might be. Vegan Shaman still didn't know.

"Leave my nephew alone!" John piped up, stepping into the room. He dropped the bones and crouched by the side of the bed, repeating prayers, begging the spirit to move on.

Vegan Shaman couldn't think through Ruby's growling and John's pleas. He stepped back and slid down the wall.

Continued searching through the black book. He found a passage written in Mother Shaman's scrawl. The words looked important, and he studied them, his eyes straining to decode the poor handwriting.

Harry's body started clucking when he realised it couldn't move. No creature on the planet enjoyed being held against its will, and the chicken was no different. Ruby began to bark again, and Harry's chicken eyes glared across the room at her.

Vegan Shaman ignored the noises around him and breathed. *Stay calm*, he told himself. *Harry needs you.*

Some of the words jumped out at him from the page. He started to get a sense of the message. *Everything has language if you listen hard enough*, it read. *It's not a human invention. Nonverbal language devices can be universal.*

The words sank into Vegan Shaman, and he recalled the scratching in Harry's apartment. It seemed like chaos at the time, but could it have been a message?

John looked over his shoulder in Vegan Shaman's direction. His words were inaudible over the barking, which seemed to come straight from Vegan Shaman's mind. He looked up at Harry's uncle and smiled.

"What are you smiling at?" John asked. "My nephew is dying in there!"

"I have an idea," he said. "Can you do something about that dog?"

John looked around. "What dog?"

"Just tell Ruby to be quiet," Vegan Shaman replied. He was surprised that John couldn't see or hear the spirit, for that matter. His soul must be very clogged. It was a sign that this man before him wasn't the cleanest. That was a discussion for later, though. Right now, he has a phone call to make.

The phone rang once. "Vegan, my darling," a soft voice said.

"Hi, Mama," the Vegan Shaman said with a smile. Despite the situation at hand, her voice comforted him.

"You sound tense. What's wrong?"

Almost in tears, Vegan Shaman told her the story of Harry Peck. He knew his tone told Mama Shaman all she needed to know. A young man was possessed by the angry spirit of a chicken, and her son – by circumstance rather than blood – had feelings for that young man.

"I know you gave up the shaman way," Vegan Shaman continued, "but I need your help."

"What do you need me to do?" she replied without hesitation.

"I think the chicken has been trying to communicate with Harry through scratches in his apartment. But we're at his uncle's farm, and Harry's tied to the bed."

Mama Shaman asked for Harry's address and told Vegan Shaman she'd call back in twenty minutes with a translation.

He hung up and stood, relieved that a plan was in place. After explaining things to Harry's uncle, who nodded but did not seem to understand, the Vegan Shaman approached the bed. Harry clucked and brrrked in anger, tugging at the shackles with inhuman strength. The chicken's spirit continued to draw power from the land on which it had been killed.

Come on, Mama, Vegan Shaman thought. *We're running out of time.*

"Harry." He positioned himself above Harry's body. "I know you're in there."

The chicken jerked Harry's neck back and forth, shrieking as Vegan Shaman demanded to speak to Harry. Vegan Shaman reached into his pocket for the lemon he'd stashed for an emergency.

As he held it up to Harry's face, the scent wafted towards his nose, and the chicken squirmed in pain. As Vegan Shaman held the lemon closer, Harry's face began to break out in hives and burns.

From behind him, Uncle John cried, "You're hurting him!"

"Get over there and keep calling for Harry," Vegan Shaman ordered him, pointing to the other side of the bed.

Uncle John stumbled around the bed and reached for Harry's hand again. As he was told, he called for Harry, begging his nephew to fight the chicken and reclaim his body.

Vegan Shaman climbed onto the bed and stood over Harry's body with the lemon close to his face. "I demand you leave this body!"

The chicken squirmed again as welts appeared on Harry's arms and chest. A patch of skin on his stomach sprouted auburn feathers. Vegan Shaman knew he could only hold the chicken at bay for so long. It wouldn't be enough to draw the spirit out.

He tore the lemon open, letting the yellow juice dribble onto Harry's face. It burned him, acid to the possessed skin. He repeated the order to leave Harry's body, but the chicken banged Harry's head against the headboard, clucking and shrieking as it stared back at him in defiance. More feathers spread across Harry's body.

Time is running out.

The rank juice pooled around Harry's belly button, and Vegan Shaman heard the gurgle of stomach acid. Saw the reflex in Harry's throat as his mouth opened. He shielded his face as Harry unleashed a thick orange goo over him, the substance sinking into his pores. John raced back from the vomitus site, careful not to get any on his clothes. He raised his hands over his eyes as if everything would disappear if he tried hard enough.

Harry kept going, an unending stream of orange goo shooting from his mouth and soaking the bedsheets and mattress. An autumnal glow filled the room. *Harvesttime,* thought the Vegan Shaman as he climbed off the bed. He wiped clear his eyes and mouth. Had it been blood, you'd have thought it was a murder scene.

Feathers spread across Harry's face and neck, as the beast sneered. Harry's fingernails blackened and sharpened, becoming talons.

Vegan Shaman shook the orange vomitus from his clothes and skin. The smell was familiar. *Egg yolk.*

The chicken was playing games now. Having fun with the new body.

Drenched and sticky, Vegan Shaman approached the bed once more, the lemon in his hand rendered useless by the vomitus. His only real hope was that Mama Shaman would call back soon with a translation of the chicken scrawl.

Mama Shaman called at that exact moment as though she'd heard his mental plea. Vegan Shaman answered the phone, activating the loudspeaker to avoid getting egg yolk all over the screen.

Desperate, he asked, "What have you got for me?"

"From what I can translate, your chicken was on the verge of spiritual transcendence when young Harry took his life."

"I don't understand," Vegan Shaman said, looking back at Harry's body, which was now more fowl than man.

"Its story is all over the walls, Vegan darling," Mama Shaman said. "The chicken was the equivalent of a Buddhist monk. The scrawl is telling me that he was meditating at the time of his death. He was just about to transcend to the next level of spiritual existence when Harry shot him."

"That explains the rage," Vegan Shaman replied.

"We're looking at a case of forgiveness," Mama Shaman explained. "You need to —"

The line went staticky. Vegan Shaman yelled down the phone for her to repeat herself. But he knew it was the chicken intervening again and hung up.

Forgiveness.

He was sure there was a ritual for that. Flipping through the pages of his notebook, he ignored the clucking and shrieking, which sounded like laughter. The chicken was mocking him. He looked towards Harry and saw his arms had changed shape. His lean and muscular form had started transforming into two-foot wings. The shackles wouldn't hold for much longer.

Vegan Shaman flipped faster, wishing he'd taken the

time to alphabetise the rituals or at least make an index. He found the words in Latin towards the back of the book – of course, he thought – and read the instructions.

"Okay, John," he said over the shrieking. "Get me those bones."

Harry's uncle hadn't moved from his hiding spot behind his hands. His knees were huddled to his chest, tears streaming from his eyes. Vegan Shaman couldn't resist shaking his head in disappointment.

"Get the bones!" he ordered again.

The man crawled to the door and grabbed the bones. He stood up, triumphant that he'd helped, and took them to Vegan Shaman, standing close behind as the shaman turned back to Harry.

The flapping and struggling had become too much for the shackles. They snapped with an underwhelming crack, like a rubber band under too much strain. The chicken's wings were free, flapping at Harry's still-human feet. The wings were unnatural, sharp. The chicken freed Harry's bottom half and flapped towards the bedroom window.

"Don't let it get away!" Vegan Shaman exclaimed as the window smashed and the half-human, half-chicken monstrosity leaped into the world.

Vegan Shaman gave credit where credit was due, and as the chicken-man crashed into the ground below, he had to give it credit. The will to survive was strong in that one. He grabbed John's collar and dragged him along as he raced towards the front door, leaving Ruby and her incessant barking behind. He had all the equipment for the ritual in his car.

He counted his lucky stars that the half-chicken monster was too heavy to fly. It ran around the farm, heading to a creek at the edge of John's property. If they hurried, they could catch up and perform the ritual. The two men climbed into Vegan Shaman's car. Vegan Shaman accelerated fast, fishtailing against the gravel, leaving a plume of dirt in the air behind them.

"What are we doing?" John asked, clutching the safety handle for dear life.

"We can beat this thing," was all the Vegan Shaman could say. He kept his eyes peeled, scanning the farm for the chicken.

The old car had no shock absorbers, so they bounced up and down with each bump and rock they ran over. John smacked his head against the passenger window, and, despite his own aching head, Vegan Shaman found time to smile.

Poor Uncle John, he thought. *He really does have no idea.*

The car approached the chicken, which was dipping its beak into the creek.

"That's not hygienic." Uncle John's voice was soft, but the disgust was loud and clear.

Vegan Shaman parked the car and raced to the boot. He rummaged through a mess of items, pulling out a rose, a red pen, and a black marker. He needed these items for the ritual and a notebook, which he stuffed into his breast pocket. And one more thing: a handful of feathers.

"Crap," he moaned, knowing what needed to be done. "This is not how I imagined my day turning out."

Vegan Shaman hurried to the chicken's side. The transformation was almost complete. He reached for some of the feathers. The chicken stepped back and swung a wing like a boxer in a revenge match. It caught Vegan Shaman in the face, the feathers sharp. Another battle scar for the memory bank.

He punched the chicken, landing a fist in what he thought was its chest. It stumbled a few steps, and Vegan Shaman tackled the beast to the ground. The chicken shrieked as it fought the shaman off and squealed as he tore out a handful of its auburn feathers.

The last piece.

Quick as a whip, Vegan Shaman rushed back to the car, ignoring John, who watched from the safety of the passenger seat. The chicken monster was right on Vegan Shaman's tail, pounding the grass as it ran towards him. Vengeance in its eyes.

"Help me, John. Keep that thing busy!"

As it turned out, Harry's uncle was great at pretending to be deaf. He sat unmoving in the car, peering through the windshield like a scared child.

Vegan Shaman knew he had to act fast. Cursing John's cowardice, he grabbed the rose – the first piece for the ritual. Tore petals from it, shouting for forgiveness with each one. When all the petals were lying amongst the grass, he reached for his notebook and scrawled in red pen what he was asking forgiveness for. The ritual stated he needed to cross that out with the black marker, place the writing amongst the handful of feathers – and burn it all in an open area.

"Shit, shit, shit." He hadn't seen the part about burning.

Searching his trunk and his coat, Vegan Shaman turned up empty.

He saw the chicken approach from the corner of his eye, shrieking as its transformed feet tore at the grass. Vegan Shaman was turning to face the creature, ready for round two, when John appeared behind it.

He let out an almighty cry as his fists came down on the chicken. He had found a spine and was using it to push the chicken to the ground. The chicken clawed and struggled as John sat atop it, tearing at feathers and catching several pecks to the face and neck.

"Hurry, Vegan Shaman," John called as he caught the monster in a headlock.

"I need fire," he called back.

"Cigarette lighter in the car!"

Of course! He ran to the car and pressed the lighter. Waiting for it to pop out was like waiting for Christmas morning. All the promises it held were just too much.

The lighter popped, hot and ready to burn the hell out of these feathers. Vegan Shaman grabbed it, tore the paper from his notebook, and held it over the lighter. The paper started to crisp and burn. Vegan Shaman dropped the feathers into the fire, watching with delight as they singed and twisted in the heat.

Two more steps, and this would all be over.

John lost his grip on the stranglehold, and the gallinaceous beast tore free, pecking at his eye. Vegan Shaman saw blood hemorrhaging from the site and Harry's uncle lying back in the grass, holding his eye and screaming.

The chicken got to its feet and made a beeline for Vegan Shaman, who had started digging a hole with a small trowel from his trunk of wonders. He noticed the chicken had slowed up, shaking its head like it was fighting a war inside itself.

It's working.

He finished digging and leaned back on his haunches, calling to the heavens again for forgiveness. The chicken fell to the ground, using its wings to crawl towards him. Its look of vengeance remained, but it was weak.

"Forgive us!" Vegan Shaman called, placing the chicken bones in the hole. He covered the bones with the ashes of the feathers and the page torn from his notebook. The cigarette lighter was still warm, just enough to light another fire. The bones started to crackle and crumble under the heat.

The chicken clucked and shrieked louder than anything he'd heard before – followed by the deepest silence he'd ever experienced.

In the open space of the acreage, the beast slowly began to regress to its original human form. Harry was returning. The chicken was leaving. Vegan Shaman watched the feathers retreat back into skin, the wings turn back into human arms. He rushed to Harry's side, conscious that John also needed medical attention. But he would attend to the uncle when he was sure the nephew was okay.

Kneeling next to Harry's naked form, Vegan Shaman saw a faint glow emerge from the young man's body. It briefly hovered before him before dispersing into the aether.

Harry's breathing was shallow but stable, Vegan Shaman could tell. The young man began to open his eyes. He gently touched Vegan Shaman's cheek and gazed into his saviour's eyes.

"Harry," Vegan Shaman whispered and wrapped his arms around him. "It's over."

Harry tried to speak but choked on something stuck in his throat. He coughed it up and spat an eyeball onto the grass beneath him while Vegan Shaman patted his back, soothing him.

Rushing to John's side, both men helped him up. Vegan Shaman felt it wasn't the best time to mention Harry had spewed up his eyeball. He hoped a surgeon could pop it back in.

Uncle John wept and moaned as they headed back to the house, blood gushing through his fingers. Vegan Shaman noticed it soaking into the fabric seats and bit his annoyed tongue. He could get the bloodstains out later.

EPILOGUE

UNCLE JOHN'S EYE WOULD NOT get popped back in, as it turned out.

I had held it out to the doctor with a smile, satisfied that I'd not swallowed it. The doctor had raised an eyebrow at me and suggested he take the eye to be incinerated. Uncle John had cried at that, but it was a touch too late once an eye was pecked out. Those fake ones were very realistic, though, Vegan Shaman had reassured him.

Vegan Shaman and I waited in the emergency room for Uncle John to be seen by the doctor. He would be spending a few days in a hospital bed, but we wanted to stick around to make sure he was okay. Vegan Shaman put a nervous arm around my shoulder, drawing me close. Pressed his lips to my forehead.

Our bond was, for the most part, unspoken but powerful.

Feelings had formed in the short time we'd known each other, growing with each moment we spent together. I nestled into his chest and relaxed.

We stayed like that for a while, appreciating each other's warmth and company, until I looked up at Vegan Shaman.

"What's your real name?" I asked.

Vegan Shaman smirked. "What do you mean?"

"Well, if we're going to start dating..." I paused, gauging his reaction. "I'm going to need to know your name."

He nodded. "You're right. My name is Luke." I was about to speak when he continued, "Luke Skywalker."

We laughed and shared another kiss just as Uncle John stumbled out of the emergency room, bumping into the walls and shouting at other patients to get out of the way. I saw his gaze settle upon us as we embraced, a smile spreading across his face and a hand resting over his heart. He winked at me, assuring me he was okay, and flicked a hand towards us. Get out of here, you two, it said. He was right – we needed to get back to my apartment for the dreaded clean-up.

JOHN WATCHED THE TWO MEN exit the hospital, walking towards the sunset with their arms around each other. The pulsing wound where his eye used to be seemed lessened then. He'd always wanted to find love and someone to adore as much as he was adored. When he was younger, there'd been a chance. When he'd founded the Children of Roanoke – C.O.R. – John had never believed in the cause as much as he was supposed to, and then duty had called.

His father had suffered a stroke while birthing a cow. The last cow the farm ever had before, all the stock was sold and replaced with fowl of various kinds. As the eldest, he'd had to take over at the farm while his sister could do whatever her heart desired. He'd never realised how quiet the farm life would be despite it being described as such by more than a few people.

The last thing his beloved, who got away, had said to him was that same message. She hadn't been embellishing. Despite the long hours and endless chores, life on the farm had kept him isolated.

From love.

From his family.

Before John's sister died, he'd been intent on telling her the truth. Their parents had adopted him when he was nine weeks old, the same age as a puppy finding its home. John had found out a couple of days before her accident, and somehow, he'd been drawn towards the C.O.R. instead of his only living relative. Then, farm life had kept him preoccupied until the inevitable happened. His beloved had shown up on his doorstep with a request.

"Harry needs to kill." She said it with the same lips he'd fallen in love with all those years earlier, the same soft voice that resonated through him like music.

To his everlasting shame, John had agreed. He knew the C.O.R. had sent her for a reason – he couldn't say no. John had never said no before. How could he say no when she showed up, begging for his help? But after seeing what had happened and what their plan had been, John was through. He'd let himself be manipulated for the last time.

To lose an eye as a result was something John could live with. A way to remind himself of who he was and what was necessary.

Family. Harry was all he had left now.

As he watched his nephew fade into the sunset, John

smiled to himself. He was thankful for all he had despite the permanent loss of his eye. In a strange way, he felt that he was seeing things for the first time. Harry had always been a hard book to read, but he'd come to life in the last few days since meeting the strange and venerable Vegan Shaman.

No, he wouldn't tell Harry they weren't related or mention the C.O.R. or their connections to the group. Or to that place.

A place spoken about in legends: films and documentaries had been made about that place, the land – books written by philosophers and historians. Myths had been born and mutated about what happened there.

Roanoke.

John took a deep breath, hoping this was the end of the darkness that haunted their pasts. Looking once more at Harry and Vegan Shaman as they disappeared into the dwindling daylight, he was unsure if he saw feathers growing on Harry's legs or whether it was his one-eyed vision.

"WHAT HAPPENS NOW?" VEGAN SHAMAN asked as we got into the car.

I pondered for a moment as I buckled my seatbelt. "I'm getting used to this shaman-nan-ing thing. Do you have another case?"

Vegan Shaman smiled, running a hand down my cheek. "Always."

An invasive buzz emanating from Vegan Shaman's pocket interrupted our romantic ride into the sunset. He pulled out his phone, giving me an apologetic smile. The display read Mama Shaman.

"Hi, Mama." His voice was soft and affectionate.

He was silent for a moment before shaking his head in disbelief. Something was wrong. I couldn't hear his mother's words through the phone, but she sounded worried and scared. I waited for the call to end and eagerly stared at my newfound love.

"There was more," Vegan Shaman said.

"What do you mean?" I asked.

"In the chicken scrawl. Mama found some more markings." His words hung in the air, waiting to be absorbed. I wanted to avoid taking them in. We had just beaten the chicken. It was over.

"It's not over, Harry." He looked back towards the hospital, but John was gone. "Your family is cursed."

ABOUT THE AUTHOR

DAVID-JACK FLETCHER is a gay Australian horror author and editor specializing in work emphasizing the everydayness of LGBTQI+ individuals. His short fiction has appeared in such anthologies as *The Earth Bleeds at Night* and *It Calls from the Veil*. His debut novel, *Raven's Creek*, was a 2023 Bookstagram Winner for LGBTQ+ Novel of the Year. Fletcher is also the co-founder of Slashic Horror Press, an emerging queer indie press focused on promoting under-represented voices—and stories—in horror and dark fiction.